NOMAD'S ISLAND

NOMAD'S ISLAND

DEREK E. KEELING

SALEM, OREGON

Published by Dare Ric Media
Salem, Oregon

First Edition 2019

This is a work of fiction. Names, characters, places, and incidents are either the product of the author's imagination or are used fictitiously. Any resemblance to actual persons, living or dead, events, or locales, is entirely coincidental.

Cover Design: Brent Diskin

ISBN: 978-1-792-78453-8

Printed in the United States of America

10 9 8 7 6 5 4 3 2 1

For my wife, Kyrié, and my daughter, Daphne. Thank you for being endlessly supportive and a constant source of inspiration. I love you both so very much. Always believe in unicorns.

CHAPTER ONE

At some point in everyone's life, an adventure so grand should be embarked upon that it shakes the fabric of one's own self. The type of adventure is different for each person. My particular experience, however, was so resounding that even the ghosts of fate didn't see it coming.

I always knew that I wanted to sail the ocean and, in some delusional fantasy, become shipwrecked on a deserted island. I pictured coconuts, white sand, fresh fish, and beautiful sunsets. I pictured freedom and isolation. It was the kind of things that I dreamt of as I drifted off into sleep.

It wasn't that I didn't want to be around people, I did, I liked them. I just preferred being alone and taking care of myself and only myself. Having to deal with other people and their problems and lives was a bore, and majority of the time, something I could care less about. I grew up reading books about people being lost at sea or stranded on a deserted island, having to fend for themselves, getting back to nature, and becoming better because of it.

These books fueled my yearning for solitude. They allowed my imagination to dream up exotic locales that were only as far away as a few gusts of wind in the sails. Reality, though, and being in the 21st century, has made dreams of exploration, sailing uncharted waters, and grand adventures practically impossible. The books romanticized something that's unobtainable in this modern age. The maps are filled in from edge to edge. Every grain of sand accounted for and no grand adventures left to be had. Sure, you can easily go out and pay for some guided tour, but nothing raw and pure. I wanted pirates and wooden ships, danger and survival. I wanted something more than just an extreme ride at the newest theme park.

Of course, my family and friends all thought I was crazy. They would simply tell me to go skydiving, camping, mountain climbing, or something dull like that. They didn't understand that true adventure isn't planned out with a false sense of danger. In fact, it's the complete opposite of that. It's surprise, it's death possibly being right around the corner, that the breath inside your lungs could be the last you ever take. True and pure adventure is something given to you and not purchased with paper and coin. Besides, I had been camping numerous times. I would generally head out to the beach and camp right above the high tide line. I would go by myself, dance with the sea, and breathe deep the salted air. But at night I would climb into my little tent, crawl into my sleeping bag, and fall asleep soundly, knowing that a grocery store and help was just a few minutes away. I had even went on a deep woods camping trip, where help wasn't just a minute away. My mother had insisted on me taking a satellite phone and using it at the first possible sign of danger. I almost decided to leave it at home, but at the last moment I tossed it in my bag, just in case. The woods I was going to camp in was in the midst of winter, with practically nothing wild to eat, unless you had a rifle and shot an elk. I did not have a rifle. So I decided to take the phone on the off chance that something terrible happened. Thankfully, it didn't.

I wanted adventure, but I didn't want the danger that came with it. I wanted a lifeline, something to grasp onto to ensure that if I didn't have the gall that I could simply press a button and help would be on its way. I realized though, that is not true adventure. That is modern camping. And while it was still a lot of fun and quite liberating, I still felt as though I was cheating. I felt that if I was to have true adventure I needed to branch out, head somewhere that would be far away from anyone that I knew.

I did some research and found an island in the South Pacific that was populated enough to get to by plane. An island called Rarotonga, located in the Cook Islands, was just the place I needed to go to start my adventure. I planned on arriving there and finding some small vessel to take me to a deserted island with no people. I wasn't going to bring any food, water, or major supplies. The only things that I was going to bring with me would be a small satchel containing my favorite knife and two books. I would also bring along my favorite rock. I always kept a small rock in my pocket and would constantly fiddle with it when I became anxious. It was a sort of adult security blanket. It was a small piece of amethyst. I'd had it for years. It began as a sort of rough rock, but from all the anxious years as a teen and young adult, it had since become smooth. It had helped me through a lot of hard times. Funny, how something as simple as a small rock could ease the nervousness that would sometimes course its way through my body like a ravenous virus.

3

I worked for months coming up with enough money to get to Rarotonga. After doing odd jobs I managed to save the money for the plane ticket and a few hundred bucks to bribe some fisherman to take me to a deserted island. I bought a roundtrip ticket, as I did want to get back home eventually. I would use that as a bookmark in one of my books.

I wanted adventure so badly that I was willing to travel around the world, just to a starting point on the off-chance that someone would purposely leave me on an island by myself, and hope that they would return at some point. I figured that I could be on the island for a month and then have the same fisherman return to bring me back to Rarotonga. It seemed like a good amount of time. I figured that if adventure didn't happen in that time, then I was just destined to be stuck in a life of dull and endless day to day work like the rest of the world.

Little did I know, my grand adventure was just around the corner, but nothing like I thought it would be.

CHAPTER TWO

"We're going to fatten you up," my mother said. Her voice was cheerful but I could see that her eyes were laced with worry and fear. "You know, your father and I talked and we have decided to give you some money for your trip."

"Mom, I don't need any more money," I said. "I already have enough to persuade a ship to take me to an island. And besides, it would defeat the purpose of my trip to have more."

"Listen, Damon, we want you to have this money just in case," my father said in his stern voice. It was the voice I only heard on very serious occasion. It meant business. "You don't have to spend it on anything, just keep it with you if it hits the fan."

"But it's really..."

"You're taking it and that's final," my father said. He waved his hands through the air to symbolize he was done talking about it. I

5

fidgeted with the rock between my fingertips, as I often did when he would get serious.

"This may be your last good meal for a while, you know," my mom said. "So eat up."

I nodded, twirled some pasta onto my fork, and shoveled the pile of fettuccine into my mouth. It was my favorite and was the only food that I would miss. My parents knew that it was my favorite and chose a place that served it not only to treat me but to also remind me that the wild did not have Alfredo sauce and pasta.

They were worried, I could see it by the way they acted. Normally, when I would tell them of some camping trip, they would be excited for me and act as if it would be good for me to get out there and experience life. But not with this trip. I got more cautionary tales about dehydration, starvation, loneliness, and disease than I ever thought I would. I could understand, though. I was going away, out of their reach, out of contact for over a month.

"What time does your plane leave tomorrow?" my father asked.

"10:00 in the morning," I answered.

"What kind of name is Roar-o-tongue-go?" my dad asked. His pronunciation of the island was terrible, but he emphasized it just to see me smile.

"It's Rarotonga, dad," I said with a smile that seemed to satisfy him. At that moment a waiter walked up to our table.

"Well, at least while you're there you can try growing out a beard like you've always wanted," he said with a slight smirk.

"You know dang well I can't grow facial hair to save my life," I said.

"Well, maybe all you need is some tropical air to get it growing," he said. "Anyway, who is ready for dessert?" he asked, signaling the waiter.

"I can't eat another bite," I said.

"Nonsense. You have to have dessert," my mom said. She gave me a sly wink and a short smile.

"Well, we have cherry cheesecake, tiramisu, and a dark chocolate molten lava cake," the waiter said, obviously overhearing us.

"We'll take one of each, please," my mom requested. My eyes grew large. I was stuffed full of pasta and there she was ordering every dessert on the menu.

"Excellent. I'll bring it right out," the waiter said shaking his head impressively.

"After this dessert I guess the money you're giving me can buy me some insulin," I said. Both my parents burst into laughter that seemed to lighten the mood.

"Your mother told you that we are going to fatten you up," my father said still laughing.

The dessert was amazing and I could barely get out of my seat when we went to leave. I can't imagine how much the bill was, but considering our order it was probably pretty substantial. The ride to my parents' house was weird. They asked me numerous questions and I answered them robotically. My mind could only think of one thing and that was being alone on some island. I could almost feel the warm salt air kissing my face as it drifts in off the waves of the ocean. I could almost smell exotic flowers, coconuts, and the bounty of fresh fish I would haul in. I was dreaming of a place I knew nothing about and simply filling in the blanks. It would be my grand island adventure. Something I would never forget. Something that would change me and how I think forever. I couldn't wait. I was day-dreaming so fervently I didn't even realize that the car had stopped and my parents had gotten out.

"Hey kiddo, you coming or what?" my dad said knocking on the window of the car and peering at me with boggled eyes. I snapped out of it and got out of the car. "Everything alright?" he said.

"Yeah, sorry," I said. "I was just thinking about my..."

"I know, I know," my father said. "Your great island adventure." He had a hint of teasing in his voice.

"Pretty much," I said.

"Well come on," he said. "You need to get some rest and let all that food soak into to you."

'Oh, it's soaked in good," I said and chuckled. He put his arm around me and ushered me into the house. My mom had already made it into the house and was warming up a cup of hot chocolate for me.

"Can I come tuck you in?" she asked as she poured the hot chocolate into a cup.

"Mom, I'm 23 years old. That's a little weird," I said. I could see her starting to tear up because of my refusal. "Okay, okay. You can come and tuck me in or whatever."

"Good. I'll be up in a moment," she said handing me my cup of hot chocolate. Tucking in your 23 year old son was unusual, but I knew that she had missed me since I moved out. We were always a really close family, but once I left the nest we seemed to lose some of that closeness. I figured I would let her come and tuck me in if it would make her happy. I hobbled up toward my old room, taking sips of my drink as I went up the stairs. I stopped and looked at a framed photo of me as a young boy.

"What a dork," I whispered to myself. In the photo I had crazy dark brown hair and was holding a box filled with rocks I had collected. I loved collecting rocks as a kid and lost that hobby as the years went by. I still carried the one rock with me, but didn't care too much for collecting them. Probably because as I was growing up it seemed that the more kids at my school I told about my rock collection, the more rocks I got. Albeit they were mainly thrown at me, but some were pretty nice looking.

I had always been interested in nature. I relished our yearly summer camping trip. One week out of the year my mother, father, and I would head out to the middle of nowhere and camp like kings. It was modern camping, but we had a blast. We would fill our time catching crawdads, fishing, and eating huge ribeye steaks. During the evenings we would tell ridiculous scary stories that really had no fright to them. It was more humorous than anything. My dad would normally start the stories. He always started his stories the same way, "On a night just like this one, in the dark woods, just like these woods..." Then a hour or so of everyone chiming in about gruesome murders, ghosts, or crazed killers that lurked in woods "just like these" would transpire. We always had such a blast. When I got older, of drinking age, my father and I would stay up into the early morning hours enjoying good beers and outlandish conversations about life, aliens, and other weird things. Our conversations would rarely stay on course for too long before something else was brought up and would change the entire dynamic of what we were talking about. It was always a really good time.

My bedroom was vastly different from when I left it. Before it was covered wall to wall with punk band posters and other weird art. But now it was half a guest room and half exercise room. A treadmill in place of my guitar and amp. A weight lifting area in place of my stereo and speakers. And one of those bicycles that take you nowhere in place of my dirty clothes hamper. If this is adulthood, I thought, I want no part of it.

I laid in my bed, thinking of the unknown adventure that was ahead of me. Grandeur, beauty, and peace. There would be struggle, for food and such, but there would be serene solitude. I knew that I could only find true happiness and true comfort in a place surrounded by nature and not held captive by the restrictions of the modern age. Rarotonga offered the peace that I sought to ascertain. Even though I would probably be going to an island that had previously been explored, documented, and drawn onto a map, I still knew that a deserted island was my only chance at solace. People had told me to go to Alaska. They said there is a great vastness of wilderness that is totally unpopulated by man and adventure can be found there. But honestly, I'm not a big fan of the freezing cold. I'm also not a fan of bears. I read that there are bears there that do not fear man, and instead see us as a meal. So the Rarotonga area seemed like a good choice. The only thing that would enjoy eating me in the Cook Islands would be a swarm of mosquitos. And while they are a big nuisance, I could at least light a fire and keep them away. I am not sure that a simple fire would keep a large Grizzly at bay, and I would rather not find out by trial and error.

"What are you thinking about?" my mom asked as she walked into the room.

"I guess you could say that I am trying to plan an adventure that probably cannot be planned," I replied. Even though I wanted this to be something in its purest form, my mind would still try going through the motions. In my head I pictured myself on an island starting a fire, fishing, gathering coconuts, making a shelter, and any other thing you could possibly think of.

"Well, with this adventure I am sure there's a lot of things that you can't plan for even if you wanted to," she said with a warm smile.

"You just got to take it as it comes and do your best to work with what you have."

"Yeah, you're right," I said brushing my shaggy brown hair away from my eyes.

"Your hair is getting pretty long," she mentioned. "Do you want to go and get it cut tomorrow before you leave? It's probably going to be humid where you're going and shorter hair would keep you cooler."

"No," I answered. "I like my hair long. Besides, it hides my huge nose."

"Your nose isn't huge, it fits your face perfectly," she said sounding a little offended.

"Thanks," I said. My mom always wanted me to have short hair. It was probably some leftover of her father's military past. Everything had to be prim and proper and in its place. But I always liked my hair longer. Not only was it the style of the day, but I sort of enjoyed rebelling against her need to control my hair length.

She seemed to shrug off my opposition. "You know your father and I are going to be worried sick about you the entire time you're gone, right?" she asked.

"Yeah, I know," I said.

"You'll be so far away and we won't know if something goes wrong," she said. "Do you remember you training as a lifeguard?"

"Yeah, I remember," I said. "I'll be fine, mom. I promise."

"I know you will," she said with a warm smile. "I just get worried. But, it does make me worry less knowing that you are a good swimmer and know CPR and all that. And to think, you used to tell me lifeguarding was a waste of time."

"Yeah, yeah, yeah," I said, admitting defeat. "You were right. It wasn't just a stupid summer job. At the time I hated that you forced me to do it, but, now, I'm glad you did." A warm smile revealed itself from her otherwise worried face.

"I want you to call us at every layover, when you get to Hawaii, and Rarotonga the first time, and when you get back from your island, okay?" She said.

"My island?" I asked, surprised that she called it that.

"Somewhere out there is an island that you're going to make your home for a few weeks," she said. "Most people have houses in the city or the country, but you'll have an island. Even though it won't be yours to keep, you'll always remember it and in some way it will always remember you."

"Whoa, mom," I said. "That was pretty deep." She chuckled a little at then pointed her finger at me.

"You just make sure you call me and are extra safe about everything you do, okay?" she said.

"Sounds good," I said.

"I won't actually tuck you into bed because you're right, that is a little weird," she said. "But I am going to give you a kiss." She leaned in and gave me a gentle, motherly kiss on my forehead. Even as an adult, there was something relaxing about a kiss on the forehead. "I love you, Damon."

"Love you too, mom," I said. She walked to the door, stopped, turned and looked at me and smiled. The light went out and I sat staring at the sea black ceiling. She's right, I thought. Somewhere out there is an island that I will make my own. I suddenly got excited. I realized that I could name the island once I was there. I knew that pretty much all islands are already named but that wouldn't stop me. It was final. The island I would make my home for a short while would get a special name. It would be like a nickname. A name that only I and the island would know about. I would name it something

12

like Coral Island, or Damon Island, or something like that. This excited me as I hadn't thought about being able to name the island that I would stay on.

My thoughts kept me up for longer than I wanted. But soon I felt the veil of sleep drape itself over me and whisk me off into slumber.

CHAPTER THREE

It wasn't long before the annoying buzz of my alarm clock shocked me out of sleep. My hand slammed down on the tyrant and quickly shut it up. In my daze I had almost forgotten what the day entailed. Once I realized, I quickly opened my eyes and jumped out of bed. I am not sure I had ever taken a shower and gotten dressed as fast as I did that morning. Before I knew it I was downstairs looking at my parents like a dog ready to go on his walk.

"You still have three hours before your flight," my dad said before he slurped down his morning coffee. He always made it extra strong, even though he would later complain of extreme heartburn.

"I know, but the airlines says to be there early," I replied.

"Generally it's only an hour early," my mom said. "We can leave in an hour. Let us spend this extra time with you before you leave, please."

"Okay, fine" I said with a hint of reluctance.

15

"Hey, you're going to be gone for quite some time and we're not really going to know where you are. We'll be worried sick the entire time. The least you can do is spend a little more time with us before you go and desert yourself," my dad said in a tone that was stern, but also had a hint of worry behind it.

"Yeah, I know," I said. "I'm sorry."

"It's alright. I understand you're anxious to get there," he said. "Here's that money we said we had for you." He handed me a crisp stack of bills. I shuffled through it and counted ten one hundred dollar bills.

"$1,000?" I said shocked at the large amount. "I don't need that much."

"You're taking it and that's that," he said. He took another deep swig of his inky black coffee and made a face like it was a tad too hot for his liking.

"If nothing else, Damon, you can use it for fire starter," my mom said jokingly.

"You better not," my father said, unamused. "That's for emergencies. If something goes wrong that should be enough to get you somewhere to stay, some food, and a phone call home. We can always wire you more, but that can take some time, so this should be enough money to hold you over until then."

"Okay, okay, I'll take it," I said reluctantly. "I highly doubt anything is going to go wrong."

"Just in case, honey," my mom said gracefully. "Just in case." In my haste I neglected to notice that my mother was making my favorite breakfast, Norwegian pancakes. They are a delectable treat. More similar to crepes then normal pancakes, they were heavenly. Generally they were brushed with a thick coating of butter and smothered in maple syrup. I drooled a little bit at the thought of a nice stack of those in front of me. They're like an angel kissing your taste buds. Despite the meal I had eaten the night before, I was really hungry. So I took great pleasure in knowing that this would be the last meal my mother made for me in weeks to come.

"You're awesome for making those today, mom," I said wiping a puddle of drool from my mouth.

"I know," she said with more ego than normal. "How many would you like?"

"As many as you can fit on a plate, please," I replied.

"I have five ready and three more coming. Is that enough?" She said.

"That's perfect," I said. She took a spatula and gingerly lifted each of the three cakes from the griddle and set them on the plate with the other five. She then rolled them up and brushed butter all over them.

"Here you go," she said handing me the hefty plate. "Syrup is on the table."

"My goodness," I exclaimed. "Maybe my eyes are bigger than my stomach." The plate had to have weighed a couple pounds, and then with the addition of syrup, which I never skimp on, the plate was a heap of calories and bliss. I gobbled them down quicker than ever and felt uncomfortably full. "Totally worth it," I said rubbing my stomach which was at capacity.

"I didn't think you could do it," my dad said amazed that I had eaten all eight pancakes. "For such a skinny person you sure do know how to put them away. Hopefully you can find enough food on this island of yours that you won't go hungry."

"I'm sure I will," I said as I drew in a deep breath and exhaled with fullness.

"Well, it's about time to go. If you want to grab your stuff I will go start the car," my dad said.

"Sure," I said. My mother immediately started tearing up. She wasn't normally this emotional, but the idea of not being able to help me, or be there for me if I needed her truly scared her. I could tell that she felt helpless. The tears rolled down her cheeks like butter off a hot Norwegian pancake. It was sad, yet made me feel important. It made me realize that someone needed me and cared about me. I knew that people did, but this served to cement that in stone. I quickly walked up to her and gave her a hug. She gripped me tightly as if to never let me go.

"I'm just so worried something bad will happen to you," she said through a stream of tears. "I don't know what I would do if something happened to you."

"I'll be fine mom," I said.

"What if you can't survive? Who will rescue you?" she asked.

"Mom, you know I can," I said confidently. She released her grip of me and the hug was over. I caught her eyes and said, "We talked about this last night. I know how to start a fire. I know how to fish. I know how to do all that stuff. I will be fine." It's true. I did know how to survive. I learned a lot of things from my father, reading survival books, and watching survival TV shows. I felt confident enough to do what needed to be done to survive, and I figured anything else I needed to learn would simply fall into place.

"I know you will be fine. I'm just being paranoid," she said. "I do have complete faith in you and your abilities. It's just my job to be worried."

"Thanks," I said. "I love you."

"I love you, too," she said wiping away the last tear that was balancing precariously on her cheek. We shared a quick glance and then I heard my father yell from outside if I was ready. I quickly grabbed my bag and headed out to the car.

The airport was packed full of people. I thought it funny how all I wanted to do was get somewhere away from massive amounts of people, but in order to do that I had to go through a horde of them at the airport. It was a mess of panic, a fever of confusion, and a swamp of hysteria. Tensions ran high as people were trying to make it through baggage claim, then security, and then make it to their gate in time. I wondered, in that moment, how many people actually miss their flight, and thus miss their chance at vacation or family gatherings. It would seem as if you were flying somewhere to relax that missing your flight would cause symptoms of the exact opposite. Stress would be reining over you as you went to pay for another flight, or explaining to loved ones why the vacation is cancelled. I guess I didn't know how they did things if that happened. I was two hours early, plenty enough time to get through all the loopholes one has to jump through just to get on a plane.

"The days of seeing someone off at the gate are over," my dad said. "So we leave you here." He smiled big and pulled me in for a hug. "Be careful out there. I want you home safely or you're grounded." We both shared a laugh. The thought of a 23 year old being grounded was quite ridiculous. I turned and looked at my mother. Her face looked like a window in the rain. Tears ran down in enumerable quantities.

"I'm going to miss you," she said. "In some way, I wish I was coming with you." A pleasant smile revealed itself on her face and she pulled me in for a hug.

"Next time, mom," I said. "Next time you will come with me. And dad too if he's not too scared." My dad looked at me and playfully put his fists up in the air to show he was most certainly not too scared.

"Call us at every stop," my dad said. "If you don't your mother will be worried sick and probably call the Navy or something."

"You're darn right I would," she said smiling. "In a heartbeat."

"I will," I said. "I promise." I picked up my one small satchel, containing the knife, three books, and my plane ticket and shared a look with both my parents. "See you soon," I said cheerfully. "Wish me luck." I began walking away and I could hear my parents yelling over the noise that they loved me and to be safe. I looked back and waved. As I walked a little farther I looked back again, but by then they were lost in a sea of sweaty humans rushing around like dogs in a meat locker. I took a breath and moved forward toward the baggage claim. Weirdly enough, the line had only one person in it. I must be unusually early, I thought.

The lady at the counter took my ticket and glanced it over.

"Bags?" she simply said.

"Just this one," I said.

"That's all you have?" she replied a little stunned.

"Yep," I said. "That's it." At that moment I realized that I had a long flight and figured I could bring a book onto the plane with me. I had planned to just check the bag and only carry my small rock in my pocket, my wallet, now containing about $1,500, my passport, and my plane ticket. I reached into the bag and grabbed a book. A Ghost in the Noonday Sun, a favorite book of mine since childhood.

"Okay," the lady said. I zipped up my bag and handed it to her. "Proceed over there to the security line," she said pointing.

"Thank you," I said. I walked over to a line that seemed like it was insanely long. But as I stood in it I realized that it was actually moving quite quickly. When I got close enough to grab a tray a security guard looked at me and said, "Please remove your shoes, belt, empty your pockets, and remove any metal objects. Then place them into the tray for inspection. All bags must be placed in separate trays." It sounded rehearsed, as I am sure it was. Saying that line over and over again, day after day, must get tiring.

I got through security with no issues and was soon at my gate. A group of people were waiting in the chairs, fidgeting with their electronic devices. Apparently books and conversation are a thing of the past. The first layover was in Hawaii, which was clearly evident by the copious amounts of flowered island shirts that adorned the bodies of almost everyone waiting at the gate. It was about a five hour plane ride. I could easily read my book in that amount of time and barely notice the time passing at all.

It wasn't long before the gate attendant began taking tickets and letting people aboard the plane. Everyone looked as if they were all cut from some magazine that featured tropical design. Well, everyone with exception to me. I was like a sore thumb in the crowd. I had on a long sleeve, button-up plaid shirt with a light raincoat over it. Under the button-up I had a simple white t-shirt. I also had on a good pair of jeans over a pair of shorts and my boxers, a pair of good socks, and a pair sturdy leather shoes. I wore these layers and specific items for a very intentional purpose. If it rained, which was likely in the tropics, I would have good clothing to cover my body, but if it was hot, which was also likely, I could easily strip down and be comfortable. I figured it was not too much to be considered cheating on my quest for absolute adventure. Lots of people wear layers of clothes, although, looking at the mass of people heading to Hawaii, my theory on layers may have been a tad exaggerated. Just about everyone was wearing some island printed shirt, khaki shorts, flip-flops, and some exotic hat that they would otherwise never wear anywhere else. Regardless, I thought, I'm already going to be roughing it, what's an extra layer of clothes. After all, everyone going to Hawaii probably had a huge suitcase packed to the brim with various outfits for all the possible weather patterns that could factor into their vacation.

The plane filled up quickly and seemed to resemble a sardine can, stuffed to the brim with salty, tropical humans that couldn't wait to soak in the island sun. I too had a sort of anticipation that excited me. In several hours I would be living my dream of island desertion, or so I had hoped. I was still pretty unsure how I would secure a boat to take me to an island, and if they would agree to just leave me and eventually return to pick me up. But, for the time being, I was content with dreaming up some lost island, solitude, and the chance at a different style of life for a while. Most people that were my age were going to or graduating from college and thinking of their lives to come. The monotonous dull-drum of day to day sleep, eat, work, work, work, eat, sleep, and repeat. That, for now, was not what I wanted out of life. I wanted something that had excitement and possibilities. Something that could truly alter my perception of life and the world around me. The feeling of looking at the sky and knowing that I am a tiny spec of life, yet I am a huge part of it as well. It was a feeling that burrowed itself deep into my soul. It was hard to explain to the average career-minded person. It takes a special kind of person to know the soul-freeing feeling one gets when they are living life on the earth, and not just being stagnant. In a way, I was a sort of modern-day hippy, without all the experimental drugs.

The plane's engines kicked on and a somber hum filled the cabin, like a thousand bees encircling my head. I was never the biggest fan of plane rides. Once the plane was up in the air and cruising I could then relax. But take-off, landing, and turbulence frightened me to my core. It was an unnatural feeling. I was never one of those kids that liked amusement park rides. There was barely a difference in my mind between a roller coaster and a plane, with exception to the altitude and safety tracks. In the case of flying, you're simply at the mercy of numerous factors. Between mechanical issues, severe weather, pilot incompetence, and sheer bad luck, anything could happen at any moment. The smallest bird could cause the plane to spiral out of control and send all passengers to their fiery deaths. They do say, although, that flying is the safest form of travel. But if something were to go wrong it's highly unlikely that you would survive. In most cases it's even hard to identify the bodies in a crash. Dental records are the only thing assuring that your remains make it home to your loved ones.

Stop it, I thought, there's no point in freaking yourself out. My hand instinctively went into my pocket and found my trusty old rock. It helped soothe my fears and horrid thoughts, but even it wasn't quite enough. I had to tell myself that I would be fine over and over again until I was convinced nothing terrible would happen. Read your book, I thought, that will take your mind off this nonsense.

"You look nervous," the portly gentleman sitting next to me said. His hair was thick with grease and he breathed like an asthmatic dragon after a long run.

"I don't really like flying," I said.

"Well, just know there's nothing to worry about," he said. "This airline has never had any problems, or crashes, or anything. Their track-record is clean as a whistle. I'm sure we'll be fine." He waited for no reply from me before pulling out a fishing magazine from his bag and shuffling through the pages.

Great, I thought, a clean record. That either meant that we would be fine or that the airline was due for some sort of catastrophe.

Hopefully it was the former of the two and not the latter. The plane began to move. It was such a calm and relaxing movement. It was like the eye of a storm. Graceful, tranquil, and in a way, sort of beautiful. But I knew what was coming next.

"This is your Captain speaking," a rusty voice said over the airline intercom. "We are going to take-off in just a moment and we're looking at beautiful skies all the way to Hawaii. Please make sure you look over our safety manual and please have you seat-belts fastened until the light turns off. Then it will be safe for you to move around. The flight attendants will be demonstrating some basic flying safety in just a moment. Once we're at cruising altitude the attendants will be coming around to provide you with drinks and snacks. Have a wonderful flight. Mahalo for flying with us today."

Two attendants came out from behind a curtain and began their safety speech. I had seen it numerous times so I ignored them and peered out the window. It would be the last time I would be on the ground somewhere I was used to, after that it was all going to be new to me. New land, new plants, new bugs, and new experiences. I was thrilled, scared, anxious, and ready to begin my grand adventure.

It was then that the plane shot forward like a speeding bullet. The engines went from a wonderful hum to a screaming roar with no warning. The plane blasted down the runway with violent force. I looked out the window and saw that we were leaving the ground. My stomach lurched and turned inside me with grave fear. My heart was beating double-time to the point where I could feel it in my head. I gripped my dear rock so tight it hurt, but I didn't care, I could see the land getting further away. It's almost over, I thought, just wait it out.

Within a few minutes we were stable, far away from land, and soaring through the sky like a giant bird. My stomach went back to its normal state, my heartbeat began to return to its regular thumps and I relaxed my grip on my poor rock. Looking down at my hand, I saw that I had squeezed so firmly that a deep red imprint of the rock was embedded into my hand.

Just five hours of this and I'll be in Hawaii, I thought, then another four or five hours to Rarotonga.

I pulled out my book and began to read. A Ghost in the Noonday Sun was a wonderful book, albeit more suited for children or young teens than adults, but I loved it. It filled me with a sense of wonder, revamped my yearning for adventure, and brought me some added solace during the flight. It wasn't long before I had nodded off and began to sleep.

CHAPTER FOUR

I awoke to a rusted crackle over the intercom and a slight drop in the plane.

"Hello folks," the voice said. "The turbulence you just experienced is normal and nothing to be concerned about. It's just the wind blowing in from the sea and bouncing off the mountains. We're making our final approach and should be on the ground in a few moments. Again, Mahalo for flying with us today, and enjoy your stay in beautiful Hawaii."

I glanced out the window and saw earth rapidly getting closer to us. Never a good feeling. Should we be coming in so fast, I thought, are we going to crash? It was only a second or two later that the wheels of the plane safely hit the runway. We started to slow down and headed for the gate. I took a breath and thanked my lucky stars that we made it. I didn't intend to sleep the whole way to Hawaii, but in some respect, I was glad I did. It made for a short trip and caused me the least amount of worry.

I was soon walking around the airport looking for Gate 23 to Rarotonga. I had to present my passport to be stamped and put it back in my book with my plane ticket. After searching for what felt like forever, I finally found Gate 23. I glanced out the window and saw the plane. That plane, I thought, is going to take me to my grand adventure. The excitement inside my soul was building, for I knew that it wouldn't be too long before I was living my dream, stranded on a lone isle. No longer dreaming about adventure, just living it.

The plane to Rarotonga was much smaller than the plane to Hawaii. It was still a jet, but could only hold a few dozen people instead of a hundred or so. The plane would not be filled to capacity, either. There were only about a dozen people waiting to get on the plane. The lady at the gate called for tickets as boarding was beginning. I handed her my ticket with pleasure and got into the plane. The inside of the plane seemed nicer than the previous one, like it hadn't been used as much, or as roughly. It was almost like the entire plane was first class. Plush leather seats, each with its own TV screen, really made the whole plane seem like a fancy private jet. I found my seat and exhaled as I sat down. This would be the last seat, or at least the last nice seat, that I sat in for a long time. So I really lived it up. With exception to putting my feet up, I was living large in the comfort of the plane.

Unfortunately, the seating was still assigned and I had a very thin, sickly looking man in his early thirties standing next to me and looking at his ticket and comparing it with the numbers on the seats. I had the aisle seat and he was assigned the window.

"You can have it if you want," he said nervously pointing to the window seat. "I'm not really good with flying. I tend to get a little sick and would prefer a clear path to the bathroom."

"Yeah, of course, I'll take the window seat," I said. Great, I thought, all this room and I am stuck next to the guy that gets sick. The man sat down and quickly buckled his seatbelt. He was sweating profusely despite the fact that it was nicely air conditioned in the plane. "Are you going to be okay," I asked? I was nervous to fly, but this guy looked like he was on the verge of an actual mental breakdown.

"Yeah, I'll be fine," he said with a quiver in his voice. "I mean, as long as the plane doesn't go down or anything." My eyes must have gotten pretty wide and he must've noticed it. "I'm sorry, I don't mean to frighten you, I just really hate flying. But it's the quickest and safest way to travel, right?"

"It is," I assured him. "Everything will be fine. I'm not the biggest fan of flying either, but we will have no problem. Try to rest or something and before you know it will be over."

"You sound like my dentist," he said with a queasy chuckle. "I always try to sleep but I am never able to, I just watch whatever movie they have playing try to take my mind off of it."

"So, you're going to Rarotonga, too?" I asked.

"No, my main destination is New Zealand," he said. "I've always wanted to go and see the nature there. I'm a freelance photographer. New Zealand has some beautiful nature that I would love to capture on camera."

"That's cool," I said. "I bet you'll have a wonderful time."

"I hope so, this trip has to pay off or I'll be broke," he said. "But that's beside the point. What's your destination?"

"Rarotonga," I simply said.

"Very nice. I hear they have some beautiful little huts you can rent," he said. "Is that what you're doing?"

"Not exactly," I said. "I'm actually hoping that I can find someone to take me to an island with no people so I can just hang out."

"What do you mean hang out?" he asked.

"Well, without getting into the specifics," I said. "I hope to kind of, survive on a island by myself." For the first time I felt stupid saying that sentence. I guess months of just saying it to supportive friends and family really led me to believe it was the greatest idea ever. But saying it to a complete stranger made me feel like a moron.

"Well that's a little crazy," he said surprised at the idea. "Do you mean to say that you're going to go to an island, alone, and try to survive off the land? Like some sort of hippy pirate."

I chuckled, "Yeah, pretty much. I guess it is a bit crazy."

"A bit crazy? It's the wildest idea I have ever heard of," he said. "What supplies do you have?"

"A knife and a few books," I simply said. The man's eyes opened to their fullest abilities. He was clearly shocked by my answer.

"So let me get this straight," he said. "You're going to a populated, beautiful island, and then going to seek out some deserted island to survive for a month or so with only a few books and a knife?"

"Pretty much," I said awkwardly, beginning to feel foolish for even bringing it up to a stranger. He wouldn't ever understand. I could've tried explaining my philosophy to him, but I knew he would never be able to grasp the concept of adventure in its pure and rawest form.

"Well, that's got to be the craziest thing I have ever heard," he said. "I wish you nothing but luck, kid. It sounds like you're going to have one heck-of-an adventure." I smiled at him and turned to look out the window.

Over the intercom a voice blurted out, "Sorry about the delay, one passenger is running a little late and we were waiting for her. She should be boarding now and we'll be able to takeoff shortly."

Suddenly a beautiful young woman began walking down the aisle towards my direction. She was very tan and moved with haste. I could hardly take my eyes off of her long and flowing dirty blond hair. I quickly snapped out of it as she came and sat in the seat behind me.

"I am so sorry," the woman said to me from behind. "I really didn't intend of getting on a plane today. Kind of a last minute decision."

"It's alright," I said turning my head around to her. "Why weren't you planning on getting on the plane?" I was trying to be nice and allow her to explain. It was pretty obvious that she wanted to tell someone what happened.

"Long story," she said. "Basically, I found out the man I was going to marry was cheating on me with my best friend." I could see the tears in her eyes begin to swell up. "So I cancelled the wedding and got on this plane. I'm not sure where I am going to end up, but I hope I can find a place to just breathe and be at peace." Her voice cracked with sorrow as she spoke. She giggled to mask her sadness, but her heavy heart turned the liquidity in her eyes into a single stream of aquamarine tears that ran down her tanned cheeks.

"That sucks," I said. "Hopefully you can find exactly what you need. I'm sorry that happened to you."

"Thanks," she said as she smeared the tears from her cheeks.

At that moment the plane's engines kicked on. The hum was less intense compared the previous plane, but it still had a hidden intensity behind its subtle buzzing.

"Oh, my gosh," the man next to me blurted out, digging his fingers into the arm rests. "Here we go."

"Hello, everyone. This is your Captain. We are going to leaving in just a few moments. Again, sorry for the delay. For now, please buckle your seat-belts. We may encounter some slight turbulence in a few hours due to a tropical storm that we'll be meeting up with, but it shouldn't be any concern. Have a good flight." The engines screamed with a ferocious growl and the plane started moving down the runway. As soon as the plane was properly lined up it shot forward and made myself and my seat-mate lunge back into our seats.

"What's your name?" I asked.

"Marvin," he said. The sweat pooled above his brow and he was biting his lip so hard it began to turn white.

"I'm Damon," I said. "Try to take deep breaths and think happy thoughts."

"Okay, I'll try," he said. He drew in a deep, uneven breath and then forced it out unnaturally. His skin was beginning to turn white, with subtle hues of green. I looked out the window and noticed we were high off the ground and making our way to cruising altitude.

"See, it's already over," I said trying to calm Marvin down, as well as myself a little. Somehow, I felt braver than the last flight. I was so worried on making sure that Marvin didn't hurl on me I hardly noticed my own fear. But it was certainly there. Just, considerably lessened. "Everything is going to be totally fine."

"Okay, thanks," he said. His grip lessened on the arm rest and he seemed to relax a little bit, although it was obvious that he was still not completely relaxed. He probably wouldn't be fully relaxed until he was on solid ground.

"Well, I'm going to try and get some sleep," I said. "It makes the flights go by much quicker."

"I wish I could do that, too," he said.

I laid my head down on the head rest and began to drift into slumber.

DEREK E. KEELING

CHAPTER FIVE

I was abruptly awoken by a confusing concoction of screaming, explosions, and the smell of something burning. In front of me was an oxygen mask, bouncing violently. I put it on and looked toward Marvin. His face was pure terror.

"What's happening?" I asked him loudly, through the sterile air of the mask. His face, shaking with fear, turned towards me and was almost pure white with dread.

"I think we're going to die," he cried out. Just then a voice came over the intercom.

"Passengers, I regret to inform you that one of our engines were just hit by lightning," the voice said. "We're going to have to make an emergency water landing. Please try to keep calm and make sure you have your life preservers ready."

"This is not happening, this is not happening," I said. I reached down under my seat and grabbed the life preserver. With haste I put it over my head and pulled the cord. It quickly inflated. I only got one of the two buckles on before I looked again at Marvin. "Marvin, get your life-jacket out now."

He looked at me and yelled four words I will never forget, "I don't know where..." At that moment a large piece of the other side of the plane ripped away and sucked out a group of passengers. Their screams were haunting. Marvin's seat started to shake. He reached out for me and grabbed onto my jacket. Then a grotesque cracking sound came from beneath Marvin's seat. Then, in one flash of a second, Marvin, still attached to the seat, were sucked out of the plane and gone. I watched in horror. Pure horror. I could see the wing from the large hole in the plane. It was flapping rabidly and then, with a terrible shredding noise, ripped off the plane and disappeared. The plane tipped and I could see the earth below, coming terribly closer every second. Then my seat started to shake, like Marvin's did. A cracking emitted from under me.

"No, no, no," I screamed. I reached out and held on to the empty seat in front of me, my knuckles white with terror. I did not want to die, and certainly not like this. Thunder roared through the air, eclipsing the sounds of the screams. Flashes of lightning were blinding and it seemed that we were right in the midst of it all. The storm that we were warned about was in fact a massive beast and not something small that wouldn't cause any issues. I looked around and saw people still on the plane, screaming for their lives through the stupid-looking oxygen masks. More of the plane was torn off, and with it, more passengers sucked out into the air, gone from existence. Debris started flying through the air in the plane: luggage, drinks, bags of peanuts, and even, what at first I thought was a child's doll, but quickly realized it was a young child. Things were tossed around and then slurped out and into the blue abyss of sky, high above the ground. My chair continued to crack, moan, and shake but I held fast to the seat in front of me. My hands were soaked with sweat. Not sweat from being hot, no, sweat from the fear of death. Sweat from the fear of being sucked out of a plane that's going hundreds of miles an hour and left to fall to a horrendous and swift death. I heard, over the sound of people screaming, over the ripping and shredding, crashing and banging, a baby crying. It chilled me to my core and brought me nothing but horror. A baby, a young baby was going through this, before being allowed to live a full life. I could barely make out a mother who appeared to be unconscious with a baby in her lap. The head of the baby dangled precariously over the armrest. It screamed and cried but the mother, nor I, could do anything. It wasn't a moment later that the baby was lifted into the air and sucked out of the plane like a piece of useless debris. My insides sunk and I felt sick, actually sick. I could feel my lunch beginning to come up and reveal itself, but I pushed it down and tried to regain composure. I unbuckled myself and stood up, trying to make sense of what to do. I looked around, trying to see if there was some sort of place I could amble towards that would be safer than the sort of death vacuum I was in the midst of.

It was then that I felt it. It was quick, but sharp. It was over just as fast as it happened. So quick, it should've been insignificant. But, it wasn't, unfortunately. I felt it ring deep in my mind. A hard mangle of cold steel crashed into my forehead.

Then blackness. . .

37

DEREK E. KEELING

CHAPTER SIX

Everything was pain. Excruciating pain. It was the only thing I felt. Burning, stinging, dripping pain. It stung at my head as the water splashed upon it. Water, I thought? Why would water be splashing me, I wondered? Then it came back to me. All of it. The terror on the plane. The screams, confusion, the helpless baby crying and being ripped away from its mother and sent careening through the air, and Marvin, poor Marvin.

My mouth was dry and yearning for water. I licked my lips, but my sandpaper tongue did nothing except scrape something crunchy into my mouth. Sand, I realized. But why would there be sand? Then it occurred to me, as if the furthest from my thoughts. I was alive. How, I wondered? How am I alive? The crash surely should have killed me. I should have died from either the impact or from drowning. But I felt earth. I felt water splashing me. I could taste the salty sand, crunching between my teeth. I could hear waves and birds and the rustling of bushes and trees. But all I could feel was pain. It stung at my head. The metal piece hit me, I remembered.

My eyes resisted my attempts, but I managed to pry them open. The light flooded my vision and for a moment everything was blurry and confusing. Then focus began to take over. Where am I, I thought? From where I laid I could see large trees swaying gently in the breeze. I could also see the lapping of waves as they broke on the glittery white sands. I'm on a beach, I thought. I slowly and painfully sat up. I felt my forehead, at the spot where the pain was throbbing from. I could feel a good sized slice right above my left eyebrow. It wasn't bleeding much from what I could tell. I looked at my body for injuries. None, good, I thought. How long have I been here, I thought? I glanced around, still sitting. I was certainly on a beach. I was sitting on a small stretch of sandy beach. In the distance there was sheer cliffs on either side of me, shooting high into the sky like walls, barricading the beach. Behind me was a thick jungle, laced with plants I had never seen. In front of me was the ocean and plumes of smoke.

"Smoke," I said out loud. I quickly stood and looked toward the smoke. In the distance was the remains of the plane, still floating on the surface of the crystal blue water. The water was fiercely contrasted by the thick, grey ribbons of smoke that reached for the sky. If there are survivors on the plane I need to go and help them, I thought.

I sprang into action, with all intents and purposes to go and be a hero, rescue anyone alive, and bring them back to shore. Before even my third step I was stopped in my tracks by an excruciating pain in my head. It instantly brought me to my knees. I grabbed my head with my hands. "Ahhh," I screamed. My eyes were squeezed so tightly to try and quell the sharp stabbing in my head that a few tears escaped and ran down my cheeks. My brain felt like it was going to burst out of my head with a violent fury. But, just as soon as it came, it dissipated. I regained control over myself and got back up.

My feet splashed in the water as I ran. Quickly, the water became deeper and waves overtook my ability to run. I dove head-first into the cool water and began to swim. I was always a good swimmer, thanks to my training as a lifeguard, but I had never swam as fast and as precise as I did that day. The waves slammed into me, filling the gash in my head with an explosion of salty water. It stung, but I ignored it. I had to. My task became reaching the wreckage, about two or three hundred yards from where I was, and trying to save anyone that was alive.

I swam further into the ocean. I knew from swimming in the ocean as a child that in order to gain any real distance that you have to dive under the waves right before they crash into you. I dove under a large wave and then popped up on the other side of it. I was making progress, even if it was a little slower than I wanted it to be.

Within a few minutes I was near the wreckage. A chunk of the passenger cabin was still floating on the water, but it was slowly sinking. Fire was blazing inside the broken hunk of twisted metal. I scanned the area and noticed fins. Not just any fins, shark fins. A couple of sharks were around the wreckage looking for easy meals. I saw that they were circling an area of water that was a shade of hazy red. Blood, I thought. The sharks already got one meal and they were ready for the next. I thought about turning around and going back. The last thing I wanted was to try to save someone only to get eaten by a shark. Then I heard it. It was faint, but I could just make it out.

"HELP," a voice screamed from inside the wreck. "HELP!!!!" I swam faster and was soon right next to the plane. The stench of burning fuel and burning debris filled the air. I swam and looked into one of the windows of the plane. I could see people inside. But they weren't moving and were limp in their seats, still buckled in. Their bodies were all sorts of mangled and covered in crimson, which gently mixed with the ocean water like some sort of morbid oil slick. I swam to another window. "HELP," the voice screamed again. "HELP!" I looked all around but saw nothing. I swam further and to another window. Then I saw her. The woman that sat behind me. She was still in her seat, tugging violently at her seatbelt. That poor woman was cheated on, had to cancel her wedding, lost what she thought was her best friend, was in a plane crash, and was now stuck in a sinking husk of a plane surrounded by circling sharks. I had to save her. I could not let her die.

"Hey," I yelled at the woman. She quickly looked up at me.

"HELP ME," she yelled. "I'm stuck." I looked around for a way to get into the plane. The only opening I could find was the giant, gaping hole on the other side of the plane.

"I have to go in through there," I said as I pointed toward the opening.

"Hurry, I don't want to die," she sobbed. The adrenaline surged through my body and I felt of rush of energy. I swam harder and faster than I had ever before. The plane made a burp-like sound and the cabin started sinking much faster than it had been.

"Oh my God, help me," the woman cried. "Help m..." Her voice trailed off as the cabin sunk completely under the water.

"No, no, no," I yelled. I had just gotten to the side of the plane with the hole in it. I took the deepest breath I could and dove under the water and saw the wreck, sinking slowly down toward the black and unknown depths of the unforgiving sea. I swam fast and hard and made it into the hole in the plane. Bodies and debris floated everywhere and I had to push the body of some tall man out of my way. I could see the woman still stuck in her chair, struggling to get free. I made my way to her, while pushing debris out of my way. When I reached her I began yanking at the seatbelt, trying to see why it was stuck, but to no avail. If only I had my knife, I thought. I pulled hard but nothing happened. I could not free the woman. I looked at her tormented face as I tugged as hard as I could. It was obvious that time was out. She looked me deep in the eyes and shook her head. Her face was as blue and cold as the water that encased us. Her body could hold her breath no more and she exhaled. A rush of bubbles escaped her mouth and flooded my face. Her mouth opened wide, taking a deep breath in, filling her lungs with water. Her body jerked and twitched for a second. Our eyes were locked on each other. I shook her, as if it would help. Then the life left her body and her eyes went dull. They continued to look into mine, but the stare was empty, like the gaze from a child's porcelain doll. The look was chilling and haunting. Yet, as terrible as it was, her face had a sort of calmness to it. She had finally found the peace she was looking for.

My lungs became a torrent of pain and they were begging for air. Each lung burned as if filled with thousands of fire ants that were pinching and biting to get free. I turned around and swam out the hole in the plane. Not only were my lungs about to burst open from the pain, but I was so deep in the water I could feel the pressure slowly crushing at my skull. It pressed hard like it was in a vice. Just a little longer, I thought, hold on for a little longer. Each bit of distance towards the surface relived some of the pressure, but did nothing for my lack of air. I could see the water a dozen feet above me and knew that I was going to make it, despite my lungs feeling like they were going to turn inside-out.

I drew in a large violent breath as I surfaced. "No," I yelled in horror. In almost an instant all the pain in my lungs disappeared. I began to sob. My salty tears and the salty ocean become one, much like the many people within the small confines of the plane, now sailing towards the bottom of the ocean. It became their coffin, the water their earth, and the murky depths their solace.

I had a chance to save someone and failed. I felt hopeless and wondered why it wasn't me stuck in the seatbelt. Why did I live and she died, I thought. I could not only not save someone, another human, but now I was certainly alone.

A sensation of sandpaper slid across my shin. It startled me and my eyes took to looking around. Again, the sandpaper slid across my skin, this time with more of a thud into my thigh. I dipped my head below the water's surface. A single shark was slowly swimming away from me. My eye widened. I knew that if I suddenly started flailing and trying to rapidly swim for shore the shark would likely attack. It probably nudged me because it was curious what I was. I knew that I needed to tread water slowly. I decided that if I waded in the ocean, slowly pushing my legs out like a frog, I would cause minimal disturbance. The shark was heading toward the shore, but took a sharp left and quickly disappeared in the distance. This, however, didn't prevent me from keeping an eye out while I was swimming for the sandy beach.

Once I got to the breaker waves I let each one slam into me with all its fury. I had lost all care by that point. I knew that most sharks wouldn't follow, and I was too tired to worry. My mind and my body could take no more. They both basically shut down. When I got to shore, I collapsed on the sand, crying, and shaking. What was I to do? That poor woman. She probably had a family somewhere. They would miss her and she would never return home to see them.

Everything about me, from my mind to my body and even my soul were worn out. I wanted to cry. I wanted to cry hard and without a care, but I couldn't. So, I stared blankly at the sea, saddened by my poor attempt at rescue. In the far distance towering above the ocean were thick black clouds. They seemed so gentle and lifeless. But I was not staring into a gentle and lifeless giant, no, I was staring into the heart of the beast that took down a plane. A giant metal plane that was filled with lives was taken down by a fluffy mass of water and electricity. We were brought down by a storm. Lives ended because of something as simple and menial as weather.

DEREK E. KEELING

CHAPTER SEVEN

I was at a loss. In fact, I don't believe that I had ever been at more of loss than I was sitting on that beach.

My body was rippled with exhaustion. Every muscle and nerve was vibrating with fatigue. I had no clue what my next move would be. I didn't know if I should just stay put or try to do something. I didn't know if maybe a distress call was made before we crashed. I knew that if one was, then people would be coming to look for survivors. Maybe the island I was on was a populated island, chocked full of people and services that could handle a situation like the one I was in. All these thoughts coursed through my head, confusing and scaring me. A big part of survival is about knowing what to do and when to do it, but I was at a loss. I didn't know what to do in that moment. I had gone through so much that my mind was shutting down.

I wanted adventure. I wanted to be alone. I got my wish. There I was, on an island, at the beginning of an adventure. "This is not the kind of adventure I wanted," I said out loud wiping away the dripping sea water from my face. I was scared. I didn't know what to do. Even if I had a boat drop me off at a deserted island, someone knew where I was. Someone knew that I would be there. But no one knew that I was here. No one knew I was alive. My mother and father would surely get worried once I didn't check in. But who would she call, I thought? I doubted that she would be able to get ahold of anyone that had ever seen me or even knew I existed. But surely there would be reports of a plane crash, I thought. They usually put that kind of stuff on the news. I also thought that they would contact all the families of the people that were on board the plane and personally let them know what happened and what they're doing about it. A search and rescue operation would be sent out to look for the wreckage and survivors. But it could be days before I'm found, I thought. I had no food, no water, no shelter, nothing. Even the few things I brought with me went down with the plane. I had nothing except the clothes I was wearing and a wallet soaked with salty ocean. In it contained my ID card, some money, and some tickets to an arcade that I never cashed in. All of which were completely soggy, unless for anything. Basically I had nothing.

I looked around at where I was. I know how to survive, I thought, I just need to get my head straight. The first thing I needed to figure out was if I was on a populated island. I looked around me for a high point. A place to get a good idea of the lay of the land. There were cliffs on either side of me. I figured I would have to scale one of them somehow and figure out where I was.

The idea of attempting to scale a cliff face was not something I looked forward to. It can be a grueling task even with full energy, and I was depleted behind belief. I decided to just rest for a while, before trying to surmount such a monumental task. It was very important and I knew it. Figuring out where you were, if there was help nearby, and getting a lay of the land was super important. But I had no energy. My body was like a shell, empty of any yearning to anything except lay in the sand. So that's what I did. It was calming. The warmth of the sun dried out my clothes in almost no time and heated my skin from pasty white to near lobster red. I stared at the sky, trying to process everything. I noticed the clouds morph from ominous ones into big wooly mammoths that dotted my view like puffs of cotton slowly moving from here to there in the gentle breeze. My mind was just as shocked and tired as the rest of my body, but I knew that I need to get working. Just sitting and enjoying the beauty of fluffy clouds wasn't going to help me stay hydrated, satiated, sheltered, and certainly wouldn't get me to the top of the cliff.

I stood, but nowhere near as graceful as I would've liked. I surmised that I spent about two to three hours resting, which, all things considered, was enough. But, between the crash, the sunburn, and the extensive swimming I had done, my body was still sore. I knew that scaling one of those cliffs would be a dangerous and difficult task. It had to be done though. I tried to determine which cliff, the one to my right or the one to my left, would be easier to climb and still offer me a good view. The cliff to my left seemed to not be as steep of an incline and ended up still pretty high up. I made my way through surf and sand to the cliff. Even though it wasn't as steep as the other cliff, it was still a colossal cliff. It rose high into the air and looked as if it was poking the pillowy clouds that framed it.

The lower portion of the cliff was smooth, almost round, from years of ocean water slamming into to it with full force. But the upper part of the cliff was not so nice. It was jagged and harsh looking. The look of it was nasty and conjured up fears of falling to my death. The thought of surviving a plane crash and then only to die by falling from a large cliff was a daunting one, to say the least.

I looked up, peering at the cliff and knowing that I had to get up there. It was my only chance at figuring out where I was and if there was anyone on this terrible island. I reached out and felt the soft rock at the base of the nasty crag. This is not going to be easy, I thought.

My first step was onto a small outstretch of rock about three feet high. I pulled myself onto it with burning skin and sore muscles. My shoes were still considerably damp from my swim in the sea, which made my footing slightly precarious. I looked around for another place to go. Then I noticed that there seemed to be a sort of pathway up to the top. It was about another five feet above me and to my right. It wasn't a true path, but more like a spot where water had formed a channel in the rock over time. It wasn't large, or highly noticeable, but it would do. I found another hold and pulled myself up. A large grunt emitted from my mouth and startled me a bit. I hadn't expected myself to do that, but my body ached and the grunt was its way of telling me to take it easy. Once on the makeshift path, my trek to the top of the ugly cliff was made much easier than I had anticipated. It seemed to have been formed in almost a standard switchback-type path. I had always hated switchbacks on hiking trails. They were nothing but a simple, yet grueling, way to get high up in a short amount of time. But with this natural switchback, I relished it. It allowed me to save some of the little strength I had left and reminded me more of a difficult hike instead of a scary climb.

It wasn't too long before the smooth, forgiving rock surface turned into crumbling, sharp rocks. Each time I would step I would crush big rocks into smaller rocks that were then sent careening down the cliff-side. I turned a sharp corner that the path offered and noticed something. The path was gone. It was simply gone. I could tell where it used to be but it was gone. Around the area where it should have been was a collapse in the rock. Rubble was everywhere and offered me no hope of continuing in such a relaxed manner. I looked up, searching for another way. The only way available was in the form of a few hand holds that would lead me right to the top. It would not be safe and would likely force me to perform some jumps to the next hold. I was not yet high enough to see a good amount of the surroundings, so I knew that I would have to get to the top by means of rock climbing. Yet, I had no ropes. I had no clue if the hold would even support my weight. But I had to try. Failing could result in me having no clue if a city or town was just around the bend or not, or it could result in a horrible death. Either way I simply had to try.

The first of the holds was a good jump away from me. If I missed the hold then I would surely fall, I probably wouldn't fall all the way down but I would end up with some pretty bad injuries. This was obviously something I did not want to mess up. I bent my knees, sprung up from where I was, and grabbed onto the spot with every ounce of strength I had in me. The rock held and did not falter. I was balancing on a small, parlous footing that allowed me to have something to jump from to the next spot. My next goal would be much harder, although it was only a foot or so away. First I tried reaching it without jumping, which proved not only pointless, but quite dangerous. The hold was just barely out of my reach. So, with another burst of my limited energy I jumped upwards and snatched onto it. It held but made a horrendous cracking sound. I knew I had no time to waste. Thankfully, the next spot was only a few inches away. I easily reached up and grabbed onto it. As I released my grip on the rock it cracked and broke off. It fell and bounced on the rock surface, shattering into many pieces. Another moment and I would've went down with it. The top of the cliff was in my reach. All I had to do was make one more jump up and I would be there. It took everything out of me to make that jump. I prepared myself for the leap and took in a deep breath. With one swift movement I vaulted up and grabbed onto the edge of the cliff. The worst feeling was when it began to deteriorate underneath my fingers. Bits of tiny pebbles made their way not only down the cliff, but also into my eyes. I was blinded, each eye filled with dust and rock. I could feel the earth giving way and knew that I had little time to react. So I mustered up the last remaining amount of energy I had in me and pulled myself up, rocks crumbling around me the entire time.

My breath was short and harsh. I laid exhausted on the cliff, trying to not only catch my breath, but also trying to rub the dust and rocks from my eyes. After a few moments of recuperating I was able to breathe and see again. As I stood and took in the full view around me I was briefly amazed. The water below was a rich sapphire blue with small traces of white where the sea crested into a surfy foam. The richness of the ocean was only matched by the intense and lush emerald green jungle that expanded into the far distance. The island was mostly an unkempt, tangled barrage of vegetation, with a few areas that appeared to be fields of short grass that rose from the thick flora almost like bald cheeks from a bearded face. I could see nothing that resembled civilization. There didn't even appear to be any native islanders that lived here. There were no buildings, no huts, no people, nothing. It was then that the beauty of the island sunk away from my mind. The idea that I was truly alone on this island, against my will, set in deep within me like a burrowing razor. I was truly alone on this deserted island. It was what I wanted, but not in this manner. My grand adventure, regardless how crazy to modern people, still had a safety net. I still would've been picked up after a month or so, but here, I was stuck. No one knew where I was. I prayed silently that a search and rescue would come looking for the plane and any survivors and take me away from this place and back to the safety of normalcy.

I knew that climbing back down the crumbling rock face was not a safe idea, so a trek into the thick foliage was my only option. The sun was softening and I knew that it would be gone sooner than I would've liked, so I knew I had to be quick and get back to the beach, set up some sort of camp and get a fire going. Tired, sore, and mentally drained, I wiped the humid sweat from my face and headed away from the water and into the virescent jungle.

DEREK E. KEELING

CHAPTER EIGHT

Even though the sun was still shining, only a few heavenly beams beamed through the thick mass of plants. It was dark, eerie, and unusually quiet. One expects the sound of animals like birds to be singing their sweet song as a journey through a jungle is made. But not here. It was quiet. So quiet I could hear myself breathing. I figured that maybe the native animals weren't used to seeing a human walking around and decided to be quiet in case I wanted to eat them. I didn't yet see them as food, but I was sure that if I stayed on this blasted island for too long they would soon become my meals and then they would truly fear man for the first time. Hopefully, I thought, it won't come to that. Hopefully, I'd be rescued sooner than later.

It was difficult to judge which direction I was walking, but I tried hard to keep a mental bearing of the direction of the beach. I could tell that I was going downhill, which was a good sign that my bearings were correct. From what I saw of the island, the majority of it got

55

steeper closer toward the center. So I figured that heading downhill should mean that I was walking away from the center of the island.

Through the silence of the jungle I could hear the static-like hum of the ocean getting closer and more intense. It was a welcomed sound that soothed me. I tore my way through thick vines and branches that seemed to interweave all around me. It made travel quite difficult. Although the jungle was void of much sound, it was certainly filled with a resounding thunder of fragrancy. Every branch or vine I moved with my hand released another aroma that seemed to permeate itself into my soul, filling my head with an exotic bouquet of smells that deeply entranced me. Scents of citrus, cinnamon, roses, and other sweet, honey-like perfumes wafted around me with every step.

I began to notice a change in the foliage. It went from thick, indiscernible plants to flowers and trees that looked familiar. A murmur of insects also began as the jungle changed, like a symphony of buzzing and fluttering filling my ears. I came upon a thick grouping of vibrant pink flowers. They looked so familiar but I couldn't figure out where I had seen them before. I studied them, but could not put my thoughts into a straight enough order to remember what they were. I did, however, know exactly what kind of trees were around me. They had long, towering and ridged trunks that were free from leaves. The tops were covered in long, green fronds that gently swayed in the saline breeze. I knew that it was a coconut tree. But wait, I thought, what's that? Hanging loosely from under the fanning fronds were oddly shaped cone-like pods. I had never seen them before, and technically, I had never seen a coconut tree in the flesh. The only coconuts I had ever seen were in movies. The tree that was in front of me looked exactly like a typical coconut tree, with exception to the pods. There were no dark brown spheres hanging from the branches like in stereotypical coconut trees. I stared with an eyebrow reaching almost as high as the tree. I followed the trunk down to the ground of the jungle and noticed those same pods on the ground, surrounding the tree base. I picked one up and thoroughly examined it with a confused mind. "What the heck are you," I said aloud? The pod was mostly green, with small patches of brown and white. The green areas were as smooth as glass, but the brown and white areas were rough like a piece of course grit sandpaper. It had a heft to it and was nowhere near as light as the coconuts I had purchased in grocery stores. I decided to take it with me and see if I could cut it in half and find out what it was after I had my camp set up. But of course, with no knife this would not be an easy task.

I neared the edge of the jungle and could finally see the ocean, albeit through a tangled web of plant matter. The ground slowly faded from a rich, dark brown soil to dry sand that seemed to glisten in the low fire orange sun. I had to rip myself free of the jungle, almost as if it didn't want me to leave the aromatic confines it had so delicately contrived. For a moment I felt like a fly trying to escape the sticky snare a spider would weave to catch his dinner. The second I was liberated and standing on the beach, the intense smells of the jungle were gone and replaced with the sharp salt breeze beaches were known for. I loved that smell. Even as a kid I would lap it up, sniffing fervently as if the salt-air would disappear or I would never smell it again. On family trips to the beach I would stick my head out of the car as we got close to the ocean and I would breathe deeply, signaling to my parents that we were near our destination. I was always a child that loved nature, whether it was the ocean, the forest, or the desert. But the jungle was an unknown to me. It was a place I had yet to experience, let alone master to the same abilities as the others.

The sun was so low that it cast long shadows on the small mounds of sand. I knew that it wouldn't be long before it was dark, maybe an hour or so. I had no time to waste. I realized that a shelter might be too difficult to make with such little light left, and decided to harness my efforts in getting a fire started. I gathered driftwood that collected in small piles around the beach. I chose a few handfuls of small sticks, then slightly larger sticks, and then even bigger sticks. I found a few very large logs. My dad would always call the big logs "night-burners" because they would keep your fire going for you until the morning. He would then add a few logs and blow on the fire until the red hot coals burst the fresh wood into flame.

I organized the wood I had collected into size from smallest to largest. I found a wad of dried grass that I would use as tinder. Everything was nice and neat and ready for flame. I reached into my pocket instinctively to grab my lighter and felt nothing. Then it dawned on me. I had no way of starting this fire. I felt helpless. I placed my hands on the temples of my head and rotated them in a circular motion, feeling the full stress and gravity of the situation. How the hell am I going to start this, I wondered? Starting a fire without matches or a lighter was not an easy task. It required patience, time, knowledge, and a good slice of luck. In all my outings I had never started a fire without a lighter or matches. In fact, I generally made small fire-starters from lint, wood shavings, and candle wax. All I would do is put my lighter to the starter and it would burn for five or ten minutes, plenty enough time to get the wood flaming. But I had none of that stuff. I had never practiced making a fire without a lighter. I had seen many shows and read many books about survival that went into great detail about starting a fire with no man-made sources, but I never put that knowledge into practice. Even planning my grand adventure I knew that I was going to have to figure it out firsthand, but I didn't expect to have to do it after a plane crash, daunting swim, draining climb, and a jungle hike. All the while, the sun was quickly fading. No, that is not how I expected to learn how to create fire with no lighter or matches. This would be a task that would not be easy given all the circumstances. But, I had faith in my abilities. I knew, in theory, exactly what was needed for a fire to start.

I remembered a television show I had seen where a professional survivor used a piece of wood that was rubbed back and forth until a small ember was created. Then the ember would be picked up along with dry wood shavings and blown into fruition. It looked so easy. I decided that was what I would do.

It was more than three minutes before I found a good straight stick of driftwood and another wide, board-like piece with a couple of areas that were sunken where embers could collect. To make matters worse, a swarm of mosquitos decided I would be their main course for the evening. Their bites were innumerable and after swatting at them for several minutes, I accepted that I was their main course and allowed them to dine upon me.

I laid the pieces of wood down near my nicely organized firewood and drew in a deep breath. My hands were still sore from climbing the cliff and ripping and tearing at various plants in the jungle, but I knew I needed to make fire or else I would most likely be eaten alive by bugs, not to mention being cold from the tropical night. I started by placing a wad of dried grass in one of the sunken spots on the flat board. I then took the straight stick and began to spin it back and forth in a way that is similar to friction heating your hands up. Friction. That was what I needed to get the fire going. I needed just enough friction to heat the wood up enough to allow it to smolder. I kept rubbing my hands together with the stick between them, but soon I could feel my worn out muscles beginning to strain. I tried to ignore it and push forth, spinning faster in hopes that I would see smoke and a little red hot ember being born. But nothing happened. Soon my endurance left me and I stopped to take a break and hopefully regain some strength. I breathed harshly and with great gasps. I really worked hard to make it work but saw no results. After a short moment of rest, I continued. I spun and spun for what seemed like an eternity, but nothing seemed to work. Again I had sharp pains, and what felt like cramping, coursing through my arms. "Damn it," I screamed. "It shouldn't be this hard." My breaths were again sharp and I struggled to fully grasp at any sort of breathing equilibrium.

I had been so focused on making a fire I didn't realize that darkness had pretty much enveloped the world around me. My arms, as well as my entire body, were sore. Bites from my mosquito friends only served to drain more from me. Reluctantly, I gave up, giving in to my fate of no shelter and no fire. I collapsed right where I was sitting and laid on my back. The stars were already shining, and in numbers that I had never before witnessed. They looked like millions of tiny fireflies stuck in one spot but still able to glisten. In that moment, I felt as far away from my home as I felt from those stars.

It was not cold yet, but I was sure that it would get colder as the night grew later. Cold was something I did not enjoy, but I knew that the tropics were not as cold as the northern hemisphere. The issue is that it is cold compared to how hot and humid it is in the day. Over a certain amount of time my body would become acclimated to the hot day, but just as soon as that would happen the night would take over and offer chills that rang deep all the way to my bones.

As I laid, enjoying the night sky, a ringing began in my ears. It began as a light ring, but built with every passing moment. I shook my head to try and remove the ring, but it did not work. Soon the ringing was accompanied by a feverish twinge inside my head. It felt like a migraine. Within an instant I was powerless. The pain had grown so severe that I rolled around in the sand helpless, my hand clutching at the sides of my head. My eyes were closed, but I forced them open, trying to evict the pain from my head. It seemed to work, and soon the pain was nothing but a dull feeling in the back of my mind. The ringing had stopped, but I felt something wet inside my ear. I wiped at my ear and examined my finger. Red. Blood red. There on my finger, was blood. There was no mistaking it. I had blood coming out of one of my ears. I quickly checked to see if I was bleeding profusely, but I wasn't. It was just a single drop of blood. "That can't be good," I said worried. I had hoped that maybe one of the mosquitos had somehow gotten squished and released their menu in the process.

If it was blood coming from my ear, I didn't know what it meant or what I should do, or rather, could do. Blood coming out from the ears is generally a sign of something bad.

I tried to relax and shake the worry from my mind so I could rest. I was finally taking my mind off the horrors of the day when I heard a foreign sound from behind me. It was faint at first, like wind blowing through the branches of trees, but it soon grew louder and more intense. It almost resembled someone walking through leaves in autumn. It was a constant sound that sort of gave me hope and, at the same time, sort of scared me. If it was a human then I could possibly be saved, but if it was a wild animal I could possibly be dinner. I knew that most carnivores hunted at night, while their prey slept and was helpless. I sat up and looked behind me at the jungle.

"Hello, is someone there?" I asked to the darkness of tangled thicket. Before I uttered the last word the sound ceased. Whatever it was heard me and stopped moving. "Hello?"

snap

The sound both stopped me in my tracks and, by the paining silence, stopped whatever was in the jungle. My eyes scanned the dark abyss from side to side. I had no clue what to expect. I had no way of defending myself had something jumped out of the jungle and attacked me. Just my fists, and those were not sufficient enough for anything formidable. I could probably defend myself against a small woodland creature, like a squirrel, but nothing bigger. It didn't help that I was out of my element. I knew all about raccoons and opossums and the like. But the jungle is filled with creatures that I knew little about. As far as I knew there was a giant hungry leopard eyeing me from some bush, waiting for his moment to pounce and rip the flesh from my bones. I scanned harder, trying to force my eyes to adjust to the darkness, beyond their capabilities.

"Is someone there?" I said again, shattering the silence. My words echoed out all around me. My focus was directed so intently on the jungle that my own words seemed to frighten me. I waited for answer, but nothing came. No sound. Nothing. "Look, if someone is there I need help," I said. "I've been in a plane crash and need to get home." Suddenly the jungle was alive with the sound of something running away further into the jungle. I could hear branches snapping and leaves rustling as each step trampled deeper. I could not tell what it was that was running away. If it was an animal, I figured that I probably scared it away. I couldn't have imagined a human running away from someone that is in need of help, unless of course they didn't speak English. I continued to stare at the jungle and listen to the sounds until they completely died out.

After a while, I laid back down and stared back up at the stars. There were so many. People that live in cities, or even smaller towns, cannot fully appreciate the beauty of stars until they are seen without any light pollution. It's truly sad that most people are stuck in their phones and digital devices that they forget that there is such beauty all around them. If only they looked up at the sky instead of down at their phones they would see a universe of heavenliness.

I remembered that I had my wallet in my back jean pocket and fetched it out. I opened it and saw that everything was still soaked with salty sea water. I looked around for something that I could place it on that would allow it to dry out. Thankfully, there was a piece of gnarled driftwood a foot or so away from me, upon which I rested the wallet, unfolded, to dry out overnight and possibly into the following day. There wasn't much I could use in it, but it was all I had and I didn't want it to become victim of sea water like all the rest of my belongings.

I could feel the thick fingers of sleep tugging at my eyes, and I welcomed them. The day that I had was full of too much danger, death, and confusion, that I relished the rest that was to come. It was unfortunate that as I was trying to sleep I began to get cold. A breeze had moved in from the ocean, cooling the island, and giving me the shivers. Goosebumps covered my body and my teeth began to chatter against themselves. Thankfully, I was so tired that my body took over and hit the shut-off switch in my mind and soon I was fast asleep.

CHAPTER NINE

"Oh, crap," I said as the wave slammed into me. I awoke to the brisk sensation of water careening itself into and over my body. I quickly shot up and scurried away from it before another wave came rolling in toward the spot where I slept. The high tide came in and I was right in its path. With everything else that was on my mind the night before, I neglected to consider where the high tide line was. I paid the price for it. "Dang it," I said. "What else could possibly go wrong?"

The sun was just beginning to peek over the horizon and shine its brilliant light onto the beautiful island where I was stuck. I took my jacket off and rung it out, water splashing onto the sand below me. I followed the same procedure with the rest of my clothes and socks and shoes. I then realized that I was completely naked. If anyone was looking, I was sure that they were seeing a rare sight. A shaggy-haired, big-nosed, pure white city-dweller with dozens of tiny red mosquito bites bearing it all to the world. I truly didn't care though. I knew that I needed dry clothes or I could be in trouble. Dry-rot, generally confined to the feet of a human, is a condition that could result in a serious infection or death if left unattended. With no medical supplies, I knew that I had to be careful and take all precautions to make sure that I did not fall ill to some weird disease that I was incapable of taking care of. So there I was naked and alone, watching the sunrise on some foreign beach in the middle of nowhere. For a short moment, thoughts about the deaths and the crash and all of that left my mind, and suddenly, I was feeling a sense of tranquility. There was something freeing and natural about being in the buff and watching the mighty fireball peer its head over our tiny planet.

The sun's yellow rays blasted through the earth's atmosphere and casted a symphony of oranges and pinks onto the sky and the ocean. Each moment that passed shaped the colors into an entirely different scheme that melded together in such beautiful harmony. I was in awe of all the changes in such a little amount of time. I realized that I had never watched the sunrise in its entirety before, nor had I ever seen it in the tropics. It was stunning, and for a brief moment I had forgotten that I was alone. I forgot what had happened to me and all those poor people on the plane. It was only me and the sunrise. The sun guided with its brilliance and my mind took it by the hand. Together we danced. A boy and his warm friend.

A small, indiscernible tropical bird waded in the shallow water a hundred feet or so from me. Its long beak dipped in and out of the water, as if searching for something. Each time it would surface after its head went under, it would shake off the excess water, with little droplets flinging here and there, causing small, minuscule ripples throughout the area. After several tries of dipping its head in and out of the ocean, the bird drew up its stout wings, took to the air, and fluttered closely to the surface of the water before disappearing into the distance.

An hour of watching the sun rise had passed before I started realizing that I needed to plan what I needed to accomplish in order to survive further. I could not go another night without shelter or fire. But that wasn't the worst of my problems. My stomach had started to remind me that it was empty. Loud, angry growls emitted from my barren midsection. They started as just sounds, but were being followed by singular, sharp pains.

"I need fresh water, shelter, food, and fire," I said. "It also wouldn't hurt to make some sort of weapon. At least if I had something to protect myself, I wouldn't become some animal's dinner."

With those words in mind I threw on my damp clothes and shoes and began my search for the things on my list. I knew that almost everything that I needed was in the jungle. I really didn't want to go back in there, but I knew that I had little choice. Generally, jungles are filled with things that can aid in survival. I knew this to be true, but something just kind of creeped me out about the whole thing. What if that thing is in there, I thought, waiting for me? I wasn't sure what I heard the night before, stalking me from the jungle's edge, but I didn't want to find out. I figured if I could at least have some sort of heavy stick to protect myself it would be better than just my mealy fists.

The beach offered many choices for a good stick. Lots of driftwood had washed ashore, and most of it was quite smooth from years of being shaped by the water. I found a good sized staff and gave it a thwack against the ground. It held nicely and became my first line of defense against anything that wanted me as its meal, or, with any luck, anything that I wanted to become my meal. Hopefully, I thought, I won't have to use it.

My first plan of action was to find something to eat. It's weird how hunger can take control of your mind in such a short amount of time. All I could think about was food. I would've given anything for a big juicy hamburger or a nice plate of Alfredo. In that moment, I had to decide if I wanted to go into the jungle and look for food, or spend my time making a fishing pole or net and stick to the beaches. I ended up choosing the jungle as I didn't have the strength to make a pole or net, let alone the supplies to furnish such a tool.

I stood at the fringe of the jungle, hoping that I wouldn't run across some dangerous animal or bug. The sun had just started to penetrate the interior, but it was still very dark under the thick canopy of trees and vines. I used my stick to part a grouping of plants enough to allow me to enter without having to rip my way through. I didn't go in the jungle at the same place that I exited the day before. I choose to go into a spot that seemed much flatter and easier to access, although it was still an interlocking web of plants.

Almost instantly as I took my first step into the jungle my sense of smell was overwhelmed by the intensity of the plants. The humidity seemed to make the smell more alive and acute. It wasn't a bad smell, it was just a thick smell. So thick, in fact, that it seemed to visually hang in the air like a dense fog. Aside from the smell, the jungle was alive with the song of birds, insects, and other unknown sounds. As I gazed around me I could see numerous birds jumping and flying around, from tree to tree, parting and moving further into the jungle as I went deeper into their homes. On the jungle floor, insects scattered about, hopping and flittering, making tiny tap sounds as they collided with fallen branches and other debris. I noticed a couple of large rat-like rodents scurrying about the jungle floor, searching for discarded food, but quickly running off when they noticed me, an intruder. I hoped that I wouldn't have to resort to eating vermin, but if there was nothing else, they would suffice.

Progress through the jungle was slow. Between the plants that were living, entangling anything they could get their grip on, and the dead plants on the jungle floor, making every step seem squishy, I was moving at a very slow pace. It didn't help that I was stopping and trying to identify anything that looked familiar. Problem was, nothing really looked all that familiar. "Where are the pineapples?" I wondered aloud. Little did I know that pineapples were hard to come by in a tropical jungle. Even if I did happen to find one, chances are that it wouldn't be ripe, not to mention that wild pineapples are generally a really small fruit. It also happens that only one singular pineapple grows at a time per plant. The ones seen in grocery stores are mass cultivated on huge acre farms and bred to be larger. But I knew that there had to be some sort of fruits or something growing.

Then I came to the same type of small pink flowers that stumped me the last time I was in the jungle. Somewhere in my brain I knew what they were, but I could not figure it out. The flower had five pedals that were connected at the base, but eventually split into their own section after half an inch or so. A single stamen with bright yellow pollen stuck out and hung from the center of the flower. I picked one and twirled it between my thumb and forefinger, concentrating hard. Then it hit me. It was a Hibiscus flower. I was holding a pink Hibiscus. I knew I had seen it before.

A year or so back my mother took me out to dinner at a fancy restaurant where the salads were decorated with the flowers. I remember asking the waiter if they were simply decoration or if they were to be eaten along with the salad. He gave me a look that made me feel stupid and told me that they were edible and quite nutritious.

I frantically shoved the delicate flower into my mouth. Instantly I remembered the taste of the flower from the fancy meal. Slightly sweet, yet slightly bitter. "A little vinaigrette and this would be delicious," I said. "Not to mention worth $20 a plate." I chuckled at the idea of paying such a price for a flower that was growing in abundance all around me. I took off my jacket, still slightly damp from the sea water, and picked a nice sized bundle of the flowers. Before I knew it, the Hibiscus plant was void of flowers and my jacket was piled high with my breakfast, lunch, and dinner.

I had spent an hour in the jungle looking for food before finding the flowers, and knew that I had plenty more to do besides feeding myself. Building a shelter and finding a fresh water supply was among the top of my demands. I did not want to waste more time in the jungle looking for food, especially since all I could find was flowers.

I trudged through the jungle on my way back to the beach. The only thing that kept my spirit high was the occasional bite of Hibiscus. The jungle was a very lonely and confined place. Innumerable shades of green surrounded me, with the occasional sprinkling of pink, orange, red, or blue flowers. So much green, I thought. It made the already confined space seem even smaller, like I was stuck inside some sort of nature prison. It made me miss my family. It made me miss home. My heart sunk at the thought of how they were feeling. I was sure that they had to have been informed of the crash. Or at least saw it on the news. The thought pained my mind. My mom would be so mortified and depressed. My dad would try to figure out what to do, but would eventually just realize that there was nothing he could do and then he would shut down. I just knew that it would ruin their lives. They would never be happy again. I missed them so much, and it had only been hardly a day. My heart was heavy and filled with dread.

A sudden sharp and severe headache had come over me while walking. It stopped me in my tracks and a wave of dizziness swept over me like I had just gotten off a ride at some theme park. I reached out for something to hold on to, and my hand found a low-hanging vine. I steadied myself and tried to force the pain away, but it wouldn't work. It just kept gaining in intensity. Soon, I was on my knees, yelling out in pain. I took in deep breaths to try and bring oxygen to my brain, hoping that would help. It really didn't seem to do anything except make me dizzier. From that point I just accepted my fate and took the pain as it came in waves and cut deep into my mind like a finely sharpened ax.

It wasn't until I heard a rustling to my left that I was able to ignore the pain. I could see nothing in the thick mass of green and began to slowly pick myself up to continue walking when I heard it again. I froze, eyes set on the spot the sound seemed to emit from. I was holding my breath, hoping that if it was an animal that it was merely passing by. Whatever it was did not stop moving, and it sounded like whatever was in the foliage was coming closer to me. Branches and vines started to move.

"Hello?" I said. Almost instantly the sounds stopped. It felt like hours passed during the silence, but it could have only been seconds. I could not speak another word. I was both scared and curious as to what was in the jungle. I could hear nothing out of the ordinary. It was then that I saw it. Two glowing round eyes peering at me from behind a bunching of vines. My heart began to pound in my chest. I was sure that whatever was looking at me could hear it. Each beat burst loudly from my chest and bounced around the trees and vines around me. Still, the eyes did not move. They just stood there, staring at me with a cold, blue-eyed gaze that stood out from the green surroundings like a sore thumb. I was still and they were still. I threw my arms into the air, hoping to scare whatever it was away from me, it worked. But what truly horrified me was that as it turned to run away I caught of glimpse of something both terrible and promising. When it turned I saw human ears and hair flash quickly by before it was out of view. I was stunned. Why would someone not want to help me, or at least inquire as to what I was doing in the jungle? The shock of everything stunned me in my tracks and I hesitated, but soon managed to yell, "Hey, wait. I need help." I tried to run after them but the jungle would not allow it. As quickly as I made off for them I was snagged up by a low hanging vine. I almost fell onto my face, but my arms caught me as I tipped over. I could no longer hear the sounds of the person running away, so I figured it was fruitless to try and catch up with them.

By the time I had gotten back to the beach the sun was much higher in the sky and quite a bit brighter. My mind raced back and forth about the mysterious person in the jungle. What was that all about, I thought? I could not have been more stumped. A real life person was on the island with me, but wanted nothing to do with me at all.

The pain in my head still remained, but it was obtuse and caused me no more issues than a normal headache. I bet it's dehydration, I thought. I knew that when someone was dehydrated they would began to develop severe headaches, the bodies way of letting the person know that it's time to drink some water. I needed to find water, and that was the next thing on my list of things to do. Jungles need lots of water, fresh water, in order to continue living, so I was sure that water couldn't be too far. Finding it could be difficult, though. Sometimes plants get some or all of their water from deep underground water sources. I was a little worried that was the case with the jungle. Regardless, I had to venture off to find some. My mouth had even become so dry that my tongue began to hurt. My body was craving water more than it had ever before. First thing I was going to do was drop off the Hibiscus flowers so I didn't have anything to carry. Then it would be all about finding water. Hopefully, I thought, water will get rid of this headache.

When I got back to the camp I saw the weirdly shaped pod I had collected the previous day. I was still confused at to what it was. I had never seen anything like it before. I hoped that whatever it was it was edible. I reached down to grab it and noticed something weird imprinted into the sand surrounding the pod. Shoe prints in the sand. They were a small and slender looking footprint, much smaller than mine. The shoe was also different, having smaller ridges in them than my boots. I followed them from the coconut and found that they came from the jungle, a part of the jungle that I hadn't been in. I looked around for any signs that someone was around, but there was nothing. Two things went through my mind. The first was the fact that someone was at the beach, where I slept, possibly when I was sleeping. The second was that the prints were shoe prints. Not foot prints, but shoe prints. I could almost make out the brand of shoe. Generally one needs to buy shoes at a store in order to be wearing them. So that ruled out any indigenous islanders. Whomever was tramping around my small camp was either from a place of civilization or there was civilization on this island. Again, I was both frightened and hopeful. On one hand I could have a good chance of getting rescued, but on the other hand this person could be a deranged killer, stalking me while I slept and waiting for just the right moment to make a move.

Someone was in the jungle, and they knew that I was here. What their motive was, harmful or otherwise, I could only guess at. Deciding to go into the jungle where the footprints led wasn't the easiest decision I had ever made. As far as I knew, I could be hurt, saved, or even worse, killed by whomever was in there. But, I talked myself into it by figuring that at least I would be looking for some water while also trying to find out who was in the jungle.

The area of the jungle that I entered was unusually different than the two other areas I had been. It was quite open and I was able to move freely without many vines or branches getting in my way. It seemed to be a long open pathway that led high into the distance, slowly gaining altitude until it finally shot up toward the mountains at the center of the island.

The ground, on the other hand, was much wetter than the previous areas of the jungle. Less plants to soak up the excess water made for a much wetter ground. The pathway was almost enclosed on either side, and with the canopy above, it held in the humidity like a greenhouse. Sweat dripped from my head nonstop. I realized that I was losing even more water by sweating and expending energy by walking. I knew that water needed to be found. I was walking so slowly and carefully that I had barely covered very much ground from where I started.

Then, I heard something that brought joy to my soul in an instant. It was a quiet trickle, but loud enough to signify that my goal was within reach. Water. Fresh and running water. It didn't take long for me to find the source of the trickle. Near a low point on the pathway was a spot where water seeped out from a small hill, gathered in a small pool, and then disappeared again into the earth. It was just enough water to make it worth my time and effort.

"Yes," I hollered as I got down on my knees with my hands cupped, I scooped up a big drink and quickly slurped it down. The first drink was quick, to replenish what was lost in my body. The second drink I savored a little more, rolling it around my parched tongue. Instantly my withered tongue soaked in the liquid and I felt, in a way, that my mouth was grateful. I drank and drank until I could drink no more. I was drunk from jungle water and it felt good. Food may make your body happy, but water quenches the soul. I splashed a helping of water on my face and in my hair. I felt reborn, revived, and ready for anything the island could throw at me.

When I returned to the beach I knew that shelter was a serious priority. Having gorged myself on water, as well as a good supply of Hibiscus flowers, I was now ready to dedicate the energy and time to making a place to sleep. However, deciding on the type of shelter was a little more difficult than I thought it would've been. The different styles of shelters can make it hard to choose. Sometimes it depends on where the shelter is to be placed. For example, if one was in the bayou and knee deep in swamp-land, then a shelter that was built in the trees would be best. This would allow the user to keep dry and safe from the many dangers that lurk in swamps. But, seeing as I wasn't in a swamp, I could choose an easier style of shelter. I choose to go with a style similar to a log cabin, but nothing as far as complex or big.

Considering the sheer amount of driftwood that was on the beach, I had little worry as to what my shelter would consist of. I figured I would use long and thick pieces of wood to construct the two sides and the back, and then use pieces that were shorter in length for the front. For the roof I looked for long pieces that weren't as thick to build a roof frame, and then I would weave palm fronds over the stick frame. This would help keep everything water proof, or at least water resistant. The entire shelter would be square shaped and rather luxurious considering the circumstances. Knowing that I didn't want to make the same mistake that I made on my first night,

I would place the shelter far above the high-tide line. I did not want to risk getting soaked again.

Building the shelter was rather easy. I took my time and constructed it to the best of my abilities. I carefully chose each piece of wood to ensure the best and sturdiest fit. I wove the palms so that each leave of each frond created a sort of gutter to usher any rain away. To assist in keeping water out of my shelter, I made a small trench so that as the rain fell from the fronds it would collect in an area lower than the shelter and drain away from where I slept. I was proud and impressed with myself. It was as if I made the shelter straight from a photo in a survival book.

After the outside was finished I took some time to make the inside more livable. I laid out more palm fronds on the sand that would serve as my bed and took a large stump and rolled it inside to be a makeshift nightstand. All the comforts of home, I thought, now all I need is a television. I chuckled at the idea, but the idea sneakily brought a sense of loneliness over me. I was truly alone. Thousands of miles stood between me and anything I knew. I wondered if my parents even knew that I was alive. I wondered if they had even heard that the plane crashed. Maybe, I figured, they were just really angry that I had not yet checked in with them.

Being alone, with no way to escape, is a daunting feeling. I wanted to get away from society so bad, yet there I was, completely by myself, and wanting nothing more than to be with someone else.

I shook the feeling from my mind and stood to look at my shelter. "All that's missing is a fire," I said. The sun was getting low in the sky and I knew that time to make a fire was getting slim. With a deep breath I gathered up the fire making supplies I had procured the night before and got down on my knees. The night before my body had given up on making a fire, but I was determined not to let that happen again.

I spun the stick in my hands fluidly and with perfect accuracy. It seemed like hours went by with no results. Although I knew that any rest would force the entire procedure to begin from the start. I had to keep going, regardless of the stinging shoots of pain pulsing through my arms. I continued spinning but nothing happened. Nothing at all. My arms were begging for a break and I was just about to let them have it when something caught my eye. A tiny white wisp of smoke. I barely saw it, but it was there. It rose slowly from the wood surface and wafted its way to my nose. One whiff of the smell confirmed it. I had smoke. I spun harder, and my arms gave me another burst of energy. The pain went away and let loose a rush of adrenaline that fueled my movements. More smoke rose from the wood, and soon I could see a tiny orange ember come to life. It grew larger as I fed it with more friction. Once I knew it was big enough I quickly stopped spinning and brought the dried grass to it and attempted to breathe life into it. Each breath gave the ember more life, and in turn began catching little pieces of grass into orange wire-like pieces of ember. Soon the entire bundle of grass was a plume of smoke, but smoke was not what I wanted, I wanted fire. I blew more and more, and with it more smoke danced out of the fistful of grass. Then, in one flash the whole thing caught into a big yellow flame.

Without hesitation I set the flaming grass down and began piling sticks onto it. The flame licked at the small sticks and quickly caught on fire. Once each group of sticks was on fire I placed a larger pile of sticks onto the smaller pile. Within a minute or two I had a raging inferno three feet high. I threw a big log onto the fire and yelled to the sky, feeling like I was the master of the elements. In a sense, I was. I had created fire without matches or a lighter. I did it the way that people have done it for thousands of years. I skipped around the fire like I was its master.

I made fire. Glorious and magical fire.

CHAPTER TEN

My shelter was a pit of moaning and despair. The next day came quick, and I soon realized that I paid the price for foolishly drinking untreated jungle water. I felt so stupid. I knew that water, especially jungle water, needed to be boiled or purified in some way before consumption or else something terrible could happen. My body wretched and writhed in pain. The pain was confined to my stomach and intestines and it was unbearable. I was sure that I had some sort of foreign bug inside me that was thoroughly enjoying my insides.

I was also sure that I had a fever, but I knew that I needed to be able to work through it. Having a sickness like I had required time, food, and lots of fluids. I had plenty of time, but was running low on my Hibiscus flowers. Lots of water is a great way to flush out any bacteria, but if I drank more of that water, as it was, I'd be in worse shape than I was at that moment. I needed to purify the water. Without a purification system the only other option was to boil it, but I had no way to contain the water. I had no pot, pan, or anything that could serve as a viable way to boil water. I knew that regardless of the sickness that was filling me with dread, I needed to scout for a way to contain water so that I could boil it.

As I stood and left my shelter two things happened. The first being that I suddenly got extremely dizzy, but that soon passed as I breathed deeply to try and get oxygen to my brain. The second thing that happened was I felt a bubbling in my stomach. A type of gurgling and groaning from inside of me that was reminiscent of the time that I ate bad sushi. I ran to the nearest bush and released the demons inside me. Diarrhea. This is not good, I thought. Diarrhea can kill. Without fluids to replace what is lost by the diarrhea, dehydration can quickly set in and take hold.

I sat, breathing deeply, sweat pooling above my eyebrows, and my eyes watering. I felt better after it was out of me, but I was still not feeling fully like myself. My goal was water, but if I wasn't able to purify it, I was dead. I realized how much I took for granted the simple pleasure of getting water from the tap and drinking without even thinking of any possible chances of contamination.

I stood and stumbled down to the shore line, where a good splash of salt water on my face seemed to cool me down a little. It wasn't much, but it was all I could do to help until something more substantial was found and utilized. Between the spurts of hunger, thirst, pain, and sickness, I was drained of energy and ready to go back to sleep. But I knew that the condition I was in was not good, and going to sleep without water and food could mean death while I slept. I had to do something. I stared at the ocean trying to sort it all out. Water was certainly my main priority, but finding something to boil the water in was the first on the list.

The island was testing everything I thought I knew about survival. Gathering food, safe water techniques, shelter construction, and fire building were all something I thought that I had gotten down to a science. It wasn't just because I was out of my element, it was because I had never practiced those techniques without first having some sort of supplies. For fire I had a lighter, for shelter I had rope and a tarp, for water I had a purification filter, and I always had food with me to some extent. I was truly living the dream I had set up for myself. The only difference was the fact that I was stuck on the island until someone happened to come upon me and rescue me. But I knew that could be anywhere between a minute and never. This was what I had wished for, a true adventure without anything to hinder its purity. I realized that true adventure was scary, unknown, and full of surprises. I did not like the situation I was in.

Out of the corner of my eyes something large and black was floating in the water to my left. As I turned my head to get a better look at it I noticed it wasn't just one large thing floating in the surf, it was actually a whole bunch of things floating with each other. It was some sort of debris that had gathered together, due to the current pooling heavy things together, like how driftwood gathers in certain areas of the surf. Generally there were numerous areas on a beach that do this. Most of the time they are a different color than the rest of the water, because of the sediment that gets stirred up. But I could see that it wasn't driftwood or sediment that was rocking back and forth in the surf. It was man-made debris.

In the Pacific Northwest beaches get a lot of garbage that washes ashore from China and Russia. I remember one time I found an unbroken red lightbulb in a pile of rocks on the beach. The bulb had Russian print on it and somehow didn't break on its journey. The part of the bulb that you screw in had barnacles growing on it. It had been at sea for a long time before it found its resting place among the smooth rocks.

If I could've ran over to the debris I would've, but my body was so cursed with aches and pains from water sickness that all I could manage was a hurried hobble. Sea water splashed under me as I made my way to the unknown mass of garbage. As I got closer I soon realized that it was not garbage that I was looking at, it was mess of luggage.

The pile was floating in about three feet of water, so I was soon soaked up to my waist by the time I reached the debris. I took no time in searching through anything, as I could feel my stomach lurch with sickness. Bile reached my mouth and stung at my throat, but I quickly swallowed it. Everything was kind of tangled in itself, so pulling the mass to shore was quite easy, at least until it rested on the sand. Then it was a heavy and sluggish pile of wet junk that strained every muscle in my body getting it to dry ground where I could examine it.

Once I stopped pulling everything to a dry spot my body again became my enemy. Vomit spewed from my mouth and splashed onto the dry tan sand, instantly soaking in and becoming nothing more than a slightly darker tan spot. The vomit was colorless and clear, resembling bubbly water. My eyes watered and my vision blurred. A slight dizziness set in and I stumbled for a second before catching my balance. Between the diarrhea and vomiting, I was dehydrating myself from both ends. I knew I needed clean water, and sooner than later would be better.

The pile of stuff that laid soaked in water before me was almost unrecognizable. Once my eyes focused I could clearly tell what I was looking at. It was luggage from the plane wreck. A part of me became very sad that the luggage didn't make it to its destination, but another part of me thought that maybe there could be food, or a pot, or with some extreme luck, a satellite phone.

In the pile was three pieces of luggage, a large chunk of jagged metal, and what appeared to be a mass of clothes and blankets woven in the mix, and then something large and bulbous protruding out of a tangle of torn fabric. The item intrigued me so I went for it first. I reached out and grabbed at it, but it would hardly budge. It was thoroughly wedged in the mess of cloth and junk like a fly caught in a spider-web. With a lot of energy, which was already strained, I managed to free the hulking piece of debris and tossed it onto the sand in front of me.

"A guitar," I shouted, completely happy of the discovery. Even though I couldn't play, a quick thought entered my mind that I had the time to learn. In that brief moment, I was felt a little better.

The bulbous mass was enclosed in a hard-shell black case. I quickly flicked open the four clasps that held the case closed and opened it. The second I saw the contents I was extremely disappointed. It was completely ruined by the water. The ocean had seeped through the case and soaked the guitar, warping and ruining it. It was, essentially, useless. The only thing it would have been good for would be to dry it out and use it as firewood.

Another random burst of vomit came shooting from my mouth, slamming into the sand. It snuck up on me, had I not felt it right before it happened, I surely would've puked into the guitar case and all over the guitar, not that it would've hurt anything at that point.

After wiping my mouth and chin I closed the guitar case back up, in case a sudden eruption of bodily fluids tried to sneak up on me again. Plus, I wanted to see what other things I had in the pile of debris.

The first suitcase I rummaged through only offered an assortment of women's and men's clothing. Although it didn't have an immediate use, I knew that I could possibly find use of it in the future. The men's clothing were way too small for me, but not knowing how long my visit on the island would be, I figured they might fit once I began to lose weight from starvation.

The second suitcase I opened was also filled with women's clothing, including a dress that must've been worn over other clothes, as it was mainly made from light pink lace and would be completely see-through. This could be a perfect net for fishing, I thought. I continued to dig through the suitcase, just in case there was something tucked away. I was ecstatic when I checked a large pocket on the inside and pulled out a bunch of receipts and three cans of Spiced Ham luncheon meat. "Yes," I yelled. I had found food. Although I generally didn't like that type of food, I didn't care. It was something besides flower petals and I had three cans of it. Three glorious cans.

When I opened the third suitcase I felt like it was Christmas. Inside was a treasure of what seemed like several souvenirs only from Hawaii. No clothes or any other practically useless items. The first thing I saw was another food item. Chocolate-covered macadamia nuts, and a big bag of them at that. My grandmother loved them and during Thanksgiving, she would pour some into a bowl after we had dinner and pumpkin pie and give the bowl to me to munch on while the grown-ups talked. When my mom, or anyone else, would try and steal one from my bowl, she would give them a little slap on their hand. It always made me giggle seeing her so protective of me and my candies. When she passed away that small tradition that meant so much to me died along with her. It had been years since I had one and I couldn't wait to savor the flavor and memories.

It wasn't until I looked under the bag of candy that I saw an item that would help me more than any other item. I found a knife. A big ornate knife. Its handle was delicately carved and had reliefs of a turtle, flowers, and other tribal designs. I picked it up and held it like it was a gift from God. A knife is barely used in civilization, except to cut food, but in the wild a knife is completely essential. It can do any sort of task from cutting, slicing, shaving, chopping, protection, and more. And I found one. I pulled it out of its leather sheath and saw a beautiful blade that curved slightly upward. The blade ran all the way through the handle, which provided stability and showed the quality of the knife. My finger brushed perpendicular to the blade to feel its sharpness. Unfortunately, the blade was extremely dull. I figured it was probably due to it being a piece of art to put on a shelf, and not something that would generally be used in any practical applications. I knew I had to sharpen it, or it would be useless, and thankfully, I knew exactly how to do such a task.

I also pulled out a wooden carved fish, a woven palm fronds basket, and a good sized plastic water bottle. It could hold a few cups of water and would be perfect when I needed to carry water around. Under all that stuff was a odd looking metal object. It resembled a circular steel bowl with raised edges, but had large dents in it with letters engraved into each of the dents. I picked it up and stared at it without a clue as to what it could be. The letters ranged from A to G. "What in the heck is this?" I said. I happened to tap lightly on the surface of the weird disk and it made a pleasant sound that made me finally realize what I was holding. I couldn't believe I didn't guess it sooner. It was a Calypso steel drum. It gave island music an uplifting and breezy sound. I flicked a couple of the notes and it rang out with tropical flair.

"What am I going to do with this?" I wondered. I tossed it onto the sand. A small wave snuck up the beach and gently plowed into the drum. As the wave receded, it left the drum filled with water. "Oh, my gosh, duh," I said. It hit me just as quick as the wave hit the drum. It would be my way to boil water to purify it. It was so obvious I couldn't believe I hadn't thought it the moment I saw it. I was so concerned as to what the item was I never stopped to think of what it could do for me.

That's what survival is all about. It was the lesson I took away from every book and show about survival that I had learned from. What can it do to help the situation? It was the golden question. Sure, I knew that I probably wouldn't be needing to wear a dress on the island. But the dress, or any clothing for that matter, could easily be a way to catch fish, or a way to filter sediment from murky water, or a pillow, or a blanket, or whatever. Everything around could be something to help make sure that things are as comfortable as possible. I knew this and was somehow so caught up I neglected to consider it.

In all the excitement, the sickness left me and I no longer felt like I was drained of life. This, unfortunately, was short lived. After lugging all my treasures back to my camp, which took me two trips, the sickness crept back into my body and I was soon dry-heaving. Puking was one thing, but dry-heaving was the worst. All my body wanted to do is get the bad things out of me, but there was nothing left. I thought about eating some chocolate covered nuts, but I knew that would only further the dehydration. The human body needs water in order to process food, and I knew that there simply wasn't enough water in me to do such a task. I probably didn't have enough water in my body to shed a single tear.

I needed to go get water from the jungle and bring it back to camp to be boiled. I first headed into the jungle with the plastic water bottle, but I didn't get more than twenty feet before it dawned on me what a stupid thing I was doing. Putting contaminated water into a container, unless being used for boiling, will only serve to contaminate the container.

After I went back to my camp and switched the water bottle for the drum, I headed into the jungle to the spot where the water source was located. I dipped the drum into the water, trying to fill it as much as possible. I had to get as much as possible and not just for drinking. Some water would be lost due to it being spilled as I walked. More water would be lost when boiling. Knowing that, I filled the drum to the rim and tried my hardest to walk back to camp without losing very much. This was not easy as every step was some sort of obstacle that would normally not be noticeable, but when trying to conserve water and keep a still sort of walking pattern, might as well been giant bumps. Every drop that spilled was a drop less to drink. Somehow, I managed to only spill a small amount.

The flames of the fire were gone, but there were still some coals that had life to them. I added some small sticks to the coals and breathed hard until the small pieces of wood caught flame. The fire grew larger with every stick and every breath until it once again had a life of its own.

I stared at the flickering flames, my only friends on the island. My friends provided a warmth for the loneliness that encapsulated me. They offered light when my world and my mind was at its darkest. But most of all, they gave me a searing sensation of being home, in a place where loneliness was not literal, but rather something manifested only in the mind.

I pulled aside a grouping of glowing-hot embers and made a little pile for the drum of water to sit on. It wasn't long before the water was at a rolling boil. I knew that there was a certain amount of time water should be boiled to make sure that all bacteria was killed, but I couldn't remember exactly how long that time was. I figured it couldn't be longer than ten minutes at a full boil, so that's about how long I let it go for. Using a few handfuls of palm fronds I gathered near the edge of the jungle, I carefully lifted the drum of water from the coals and placed it in the sand to cool.

Looking around my camp, I felt that I had it made. The only thing that baffled me was the mysterious pod that I had found. Finally having a knife in my possession, I decided it was time to figure out what it was. With one swing I buried the knife into the pod. It landed deep, and was slightly stuck in what appeared to be a sort of fibrous material. I tried a sawing motion but that didn't do much of anything. A few more swings into the pod provided me with a way to grip the fibers and pull it away. It took all my strength but I managed to get a good sized piece of it off. Underneath was a mess of long and tough fibers. After ripping another few chunks off I saw something both unexpected and wonderful. Inside the pod was a coconut. I never would've guessed that a coconut came tightly wrapped inside such an unusual shaped pod, but I was thoroughly glad. I had seen the pods all over the island and knew that they would probably become a big part of my future diet.

With another swift swing of the knife I cracked the coconut open, spilling some of its milk onto the sand. I quickly drank the remaining milk. It was wonderfully sweet and left a sort of silken feel in my mouth that was quite pleasing. I sliced off a large chunk of the meat and tossed it into my mouth. It was delicious. Much more so than a grocery store coconut. This was fresh, revitalizing, and the epitome of an island treat. Without hesitation I ended up finishing off one half of the coconut in a single sitting. What was weird was that I felt kind of full.

Considering the situation, it seemed that everything was looking pretty good. I had food, a way to boil and contain water, a knife, and even some clothing that could be used for various survival tasks.

It seemed that nothing could get worse.

CHAPTER ELEVEN

"Stop messing with me," I screamed at the jungle fringe. A bush moved and I lunged toward it, knife in hand, but nothing was there. "Why are you doing this? Just show yourself or leave me alone." To my right another bush moved. I pounced and began slashing violently into the jungle bush. With each slash a bellowing yell came from inside me. But none of the results I wanted came from the slashing. No person, no screams, no blood, nothing. Nothing but pieces of plant debris falling onto the sand below me, crying like tears from the jungle. I knew someone was there, haunting me from the jungle edge. But they would not show themselves. They never showed themselves.

Instead, they mocked me. The sounds, the human-like shapes, and the whispers that all came from the thick darkness of jungle. I could hear them laughing at me. Laughing because I was stuck in a

91

horrible nightmare of isolation and confusion. I could not understand why someone would want to torment me when I was in need of help. It was obvious that they didn't care. They enjoyed playing games with me, taunting me at every turn. When I went on water runs, they were there. When I looked for food, they were there. When I slept, they were there. I rarely saw them. Mainly just flashes of them when they moved from place to place. I did, however, hear them every time there were near. It was clear that they had gotten more comfortable with being close to me and hanging around longer. In the beginning, I would hear them, then I would say something or make a sound, and they would scurry off into obscurity. But as the days and weeks passed they didn't care if I made a sound, they simply enjoyed my distress and just seemed to move around me instead of running off. They were a plague on my already dire situation.

As I stood staring into the jungle, trying to catch a glimpse of them, I heard another sound. I crept toward it and stabbed at where I thought the sound was coming from. Almost immediately, a large, brightly colored bird flew out from the thick plants. Instinctively, I swung the knife around in the air, before realizing that it was just a bird. It squawked and flew off. My heart was racing. "I know you're in there," I screamed. "This isn't a game. I need help and all you do is mess with me. Well I don't want your help anymore. Stay away from me or else."

I scratched another mark into the rock face with my knife. I then counted all the tally marks. "Today's mark makes 97," I said. "Over three months. I've been stuck here for over three months." I wondered if I would ever be found. It seemed like I would die on the island. It could've been from starvation, dehydration, disease, an accident, or worse. I could've been killed by whomever was lurking beyond the jungle's edge. Oh, the many ways I could've found death. But despite it all, I was not going to let anything happen to me.

Over the months I perfected the art of fire. I was a master of obtaining clean drinking water. I even fashioned a net from the lace clothing and was catching fish, crab, and other creatures of the sea. All my survival skills were honed and I figured I could probably last quite some time, assuming supplies of fish, water, and wood were still plentiful. But I was being hunted by an unseen entity. I was tired of being tormented at every turn and soon decided that it was my time to do the tormenting. I was going on a hunt.

Unlike most animals, what I was going to hunt could plan, foresee, and anticipate, so I needed to have any advantage I could get. I knew the beach very well, but they knew the jungle. Generally, I would go into the jungle to get fresh water, gather coconuts, or other edibles. But this time I was going in to stalk, and they had the home-field advantage.

"Preparation is key," I whispered to myself as I wrapped some palm cordage around my knife and a long study piece of driftwood. My plan was to extend the reach of the knife so that there was some distance between me and the hunted. It would also allow some extra stabbing power. Once the knife was securely fastened to the stick, I took a practice stab at one of the coconut pods I had laying around. With one swift motion the knife went right through the pod and into the coconut. Milk seeped out from the wound and drained onto the sand. "That's what I'm talking about," I said confidently, proud of the weapon I created.

I didn't want to kill whoever was out in the jungle, but I was mentally ready to do whatever I had to should the situation arise. I was at my wit's end. But, what I was hoping for was to find someone and have them help me. But, based on the fact that they taunted me whenever they could, I knew that more forceful measures might have been required. I was ready for whatever came at me in the damp, dark jungle.

It was safe to say that I was a little paranoid, but rightfully so. Someone was on the island with me but they weren't trying to help me. Over the course of the three months they watched me struggle for food, water, shelter, fire, and everything else that happened to me, but they made no attempts to help. Instead, they just stayed in the shadows and watched me trudge around the island like a slug in a salt mine. I had no clue why they were doing it to me. But I needed to know. I had to figure out why they weren't helping, and more so, I needed to force them to help me get off the island if they weren't willing on their own accord.

"They will help me or they will die," I whispered to myself with a maniacal grin that stretched across my face. "I'm coming for you," I yelled at the foliage. "You won't be able to hide for long."

The jungle was soggy with humidity. So much, in fact, that breathing was akin to drinking, each breath a gulp of sodden air. If there was any more moisture in the air, it may have been possible to slowly drown within its damp confines. My skin was hot and sticky, but I didn't care. I was on a mission and being uncomfortable was not going to prevent me from completing it. I took each step with care, so I wouldn't make too much noise. I wanted the element of surprise, or at least as much as I could get.

I strategically began the hunt an hour or so before the sun set. This way, if I was seen during daylight I would be able to use the cover of darkness to conceal myself and my position. The sun was getting low in the sky and the darkness of the jungle began to take over with speed. I welcomed it. Part of me knew what I was doing was a insane, but the other part was overriding it. It felt like the little angel and devil on the shoulders of characters in old cartoons. On my shoulders, the devil was winning the argument and pushing his influence. But, in realty, there were no tiny angels or devils, there was just me, the thick air of the darkening jungle, and an unknown entity that needed to be found.

Once it was dark enough, I found some vines and other plants and cut them free. I then covered myself in them for camouflage. The ground was so wet that it was easy to gather a few handfuls of mud and smear it over my face and hands. It wasn't long before I blended into the dark jungle. I was sure that nothing would be able to see me. I was consumed by both the darkness and my camouflage.

I continued to creep through the terrain. My eyes had eventually adjusted to the point where I could see a basic outline of the landscape, although details were obscure. I followed what seemed to be some sort of a path, whether made by animals or by man, I did not know. The path quickly gained elevation as it slithered deeper into the jungle. My eyes scanned back and forth for any sort of unusual movement that would possibly lead me to whom I was hunting. Unfortunately, I saw nothing that gave me a hint as to where they were.

I hunted for hours, and to the point where I could see glimpses of the moon peeking itself through the jungle trees. It shined high and brightly in the night sky, yet the jungle only allowed the occasional moonbeam to pierce through the thick canopy and light up a small section of jungle floor. In any other situation, I would've reveled at its beauty. But, in that moment, my mind was not focusing on the beauty of the moonlight casting itself into the jungle, but rather the beauty of the hunt and each of my carefully planned movements. Each step with purpose and full of grace, much like the fluent body of a ballet dancer. My thoughts were dagger sharp and my eyes scrutinized every leaf, vine, and shape in the dark. My hands tightly gripped my weapon, ready to impale anyone that dared to get too close to me. I was ready for blood.

In that moment a thought ripped through the hunter mentality that had taken over me. "What are you doing?" The thought said from the depths of my mind. "Is this who you are?" I stopped in my tracks, letting the questions waft over me like a thick fog in my mind. The voice in my head sounded familiar, but had a sort of unknown distance to it, like I hadn't heard from it in a long time. "This is not who you are," the voice said again, this time feeling closer and louder. "You're not a hunter or a killer. Stop this now and go back." It was kind of soothing to hear such remarks, like a weight was being lifted from inside my mind. Then, without warning, the voice seemed to be screaming from within me, "Leave now. This is not who you want to be." The deafening scream brought on a sudden headache that grew into dizziness. I struggled to keep my balance and before I knew it I was laying on my side in a puddle of lukewarm muddy water next to the trail.

I laid still, soaked to the core, letting the headache, dizziness, and voice take over me. About a few feet to my left a sound shot out from the darkness. It was the sound of footsteps walking toward me. The steps weren't hurried, but rather like someone taking a leisurely stroll. Whoever it was had no clue that I was laying so close to them. They were probably either looking for me and trying to be cunning, or they were oblivious to my presence in the jungle. I could make out a rough outline of their body as they neared me. They were short, and of an average build.

"Don't do this," the voice in my head yelled. Then the footsteps stopped within a foot from where I laid. The murky silhouette stood still in the night, almost as if it heard the voice in my head shouting out. I held my breath, so as not to be heard. The silhouette was facing my direction, but there was no way they could've seen me. I was laying down, covered in mud and plants, in my camouflage. I was silent and motionless. The stillness consumed the world around me. Even the jungle seemed to be holding its breath. The voice in my head continued to scream at me. "Go back to the beach. End this now," it shrieked.

If we were playing a game of stillness, I won, because without provocation, the dusky outline in the jungle began walking away. I released my breath and slowly followed the figure with my eyes. There was then another voice in my head. It was deeper and more rooted in my mind than the previous voice. It took away my dizziness and eased my pains. "Follow," it simply said. Like a pawn in a game of sick chess, I obeyed. I quietly stood from the warm puddle. I could still hear the first voice in my mind telling me to leave, but it was in the background, and fading quickly. Soon, the first voice trailed away in my mind until it was completely drowned out by the second voice. All I could hear was it telling me to follow the obscure shadow. I didn't dare defy its sternness.

The word repeated over and over in my head. "Follow," it said with honed authority. I took careful steps, about twenty or so feet behind the silhouette. I was subtle as I tailed the figure. We slowly gained more and more elevation as we walked.

I didn't really have a plan. But I hoped that I would follow the shadowy figure to its camp before I confronted them. I could then wait until they were sleeping, or daylight, and then be able to have the upper hand. I pictured myself standing over them as they slept, spear in hand, waking them up, and forcing them to explain why they haven't helped me. I figured that they would tell me and then I would demand that they help or else I would do something more drastic.

The trail came to a sharp bend that veered to the left. The silhouette disappeared from my sight as they rounded the bend. I quietly, but silently, hurried my pace to catch up to them. When I came around the corner they were gone. I stopped and tried to focus my vision, thinking that maybe I just couldn't see them. This was not the case, as the trail continued on a straight path after the bend. They were gone. In the course of just a few seconds they had vanished from view. "Where the heck did they go?" I said in a soft, angry whisper. I looked at the jungle that paralleled the trail, thinking that there could've been another path. But the jungle was so thick on either side that I would've certainly heard some sort of sound alerting me that they entered into the bush.

"Find and kill," the voice said suddenly, with a passionate power from within in my mind. "Find and kill now." My body listened and reacted according, soaring down the path at top speed. The trail had finally leveled out after gaining considerable elevation and I was running with little hindrance. My camouflage began falling off of me, leaving behind a trail of vines and other flora. I could still barely see, but a sort of panic had set in and I didn't care if I could see or not, I just needed to catch up to them before they got away. There was no more time or need for stealth.

"You're not getting away from me now," I yelled, voice cracking, as I flew down the path. "Come out and face me." The silence was gone. My surreptitious stalking was a thing of the past. The jungle was now alive with the sounds of my footsteps and my screams. "I will find you." I could only wonder how the silhouette evaded me in such a short time. One moment they were there, on the path, and the next they somehow disappeared from view. I didn't have much time to ponder how they managed to elude me, because in my mind, as I ran fervently through the jungle, my mind could only hear one voice.

Over and over it screamed, "Find and kill. Find and kill. Find and kill." It was deafening. It overwhelmed me. It did, however, fuel me to run faster. The only thing in me that was faster than my speed on the path was my heartbeat. It thumped through my chest, into my neck, and beat like a timpani in my head.

In my haste, I neglected to notice that the path took another sharp turn, this time to the right. I continued to run straight and before I could fix my mistake, I found myself rolling violently down a steep hill. My body explosively ripped through tangles of vines. I felt every rock, branch, and bump as I careened down the hill. The wet nature of the jungle lubricated my descent. The only thing that slowed me was the occasional slam into a sharp rock. Small bits of flesh tore away from my body as I rolled through a stout thicket of thorny plants. My body was soon covered in cuts, a penance the hill offered and paid in full. Everything seemed to happen in slow motion, but it couldn't have taken more than a few seconds.

I laid, groaning in agonizing pain at the bottom of the hill. There were dozens of cuts, some small and meaningless, but some quite a bit bigger. The blood mixed with the remaining mud on my body and created a somber looking ooze. My bones ringed with a weird sort of dull pain that coursed through my body. There wasn't a single place on me that didn't hurt. Yet, in all the pain, all I could hear was three words, still screaming in my mind. "Find and kill."

My legs buckled from under me as I tried to stand. I laid in the middle of the jungle, hot with humidity, soaked in blood and mud, and aches coming from every nerve in my body. With stinging blood in my eyes, I glanced around me to see if I could possibly figure out where I was, even though I knew that there was no way. I was in an area of the jungle that I had never been before. I could tell that I was in a sort of clearing at the bottom of the hill I just rolled down. It was a valley, probably an old riverbed. This was a good thing. Even though it might be a dried riverbed, I knew that it would lead back to the ocean, which in turn, would lead me back to my camp.

"Find and kill," the voice in my head continued to scream. "Find and kill." It begged me, but I didn't listen anymore. I couldn't. The voice was loud, but the pain in my body was louder. I just wanted to get back to my camp and try to rest. "Shut up," I yelled out loud. "Just shut up." And as if the voice in my head listened, it went away. Just like that, it was gone. I breathed a sigh of relief. I was determined to find and kill whoever it was that was haunting me, but after the pounding I took down the hill I just wanted to get back to camp.

The walk back was horrible. A dried up riverbed may seem like an ideal place to hike through the jungle, but indeed it was not. The entire floor of the bed was laced with huge logs, rocks of all sizes, and groupings of new plants. The plants, being as they were so small, and the fact that it was dark, were death traps. Each small plant seemed to grab at my feet in the dark like small hands. I fell down numerous times, each fall adding more pain to my already debilitated frame. I could not get back up the valley in the shape I was in, being as the walls of the valley were so steep. It didn't seem like there was anywhere that flattened out and lead back into the jungle toward the path. I was stuck walking the obstacle course riverbed.

It seemed like I walked for hours. The sun had begun shining from behind the horizon. I was surprised that so much time had passed. It had not seemed like hours had gone by. If anything, it felt more like I was missing time. Like hours were robbed from me. But, in my derangement, time seemed frivolous. The little bit of light helped me maneuver the treacherous bed considerably easier than the pitch black darkness. I was making good progress, and knew that I had to be getting close. It was then that I saw the ledge. About 20 yards in front of me was what appeared to be a drop off. As I got closer my fears were confirmed. I was standing on the ledge of an old waterfall. The drop was significant. It was easily 30 feet. I could see the beach not too far off in the distance. I could hear the waves crashing. I just needed to figure out a way down the waterfall.

I was so tired. Sore and tired. I just wanted rest. I contemplated jumping down, letting the rocks below smash me into pieces, sending me into the deepest of sleeps. But something in me turned me away from that idea. I had to climb down. It was the only way. I walked to my left and scouted a semi-safe pathway down protruding rocks. They formed a ladders of sorts. I didn't have the energy, but it was going to be my only choice. The first few rocks were easy enough, but I came to a spot where I needed to dangle precariously, swing inward, drop down, and hope that the shelf held, or that I didn't slip. I lowered myself and held on with only my hands. My feet dangled and I began to swing. I was so scared, tired, and sore, but my ability to judge risk overwhelmed any sense of safety. I let go at the right moment and my feet landed onto the shelf below me. The shelf, however, was not anchored enough into the wall, it slid out like it was greased up. I fell, my face slamming into the rocks jetting out of the wall. Thankfully, the next shelf protruded enough and caught my fall. It was only about a ten foot drop, but it hurt. My nose instantly started dripping blood. I didn't care. I let it bleed. It was now a sort of trophy of my bravery, or stupidity. Either way I was wearing it with pride. It was just another memento of my insanity in the jungle.

The final jump was easy, and soon I was on the ground again, with the ocean just a short walk away. The moment I was on the beach I ran to the water and splashed some on my face. I kneeled in the sand holding my face with my hands. I was half-asleep, half-dead, and ready for solace.

It took me another half-hour to find my camp. I had to climb over the small cape I climbed on my first day on the island. Thankfully, there was enough light to see what I was doing, as well as a revitalizing feeling of being back on the beach. My camp was a welcomed sight. Before I knew it I was on the ground in my shelter. Sleep overtook me and soon the pain disappeared behind a veil of slumber.

CHAPTER TWELVE

Months had gone by, or was it years? There were so many scratches in the rock wall that I couldn't count them anymore. It didn't matter anyway. The island was my home. I had given into the idea that I was going to be there forever. It felt like I had already spent a lifetime there. It was better that I was stuck there anyway. My family had probably already mourned me and moved on. Getting back to them would only make them realize that ghosts were real. It would shock them. They would again have to mourn if I returned. They would go through the pain of thinking that they didn't look hard enough, that they gave up too soon, and that they were terrible people. Why would I have wanted to do that to them? They were better off with me on the island. In some sense, I was probably better off too. If I had somehow gotten back to the real world I would've been shocked. I had forgotten how to act civilized.

The things I did on the island would frighten and shock civilized people. I drank urine, ate rotting animals, senselessly ripped apart a turtle and ate it raw, and more horrible things that are too terrible to mention. I was a completely different person. My hair was long a scraggily. Still couldn't grow a beard, however. The adventure I sought out became normal. Survival was my life. But it was growing painful, to both my body and my soul.

I was always searching for food, every minute of every day. If I saw an opportunity, be it a bug, bird, fish, or fruit, I would stop everything I was doing and attempt to procure it. There were times that I went without any food for days. Being too tired to hunt, fish, or gather was a horrible feeling. My brain would scream out for food, but my body wouldn't have the energy to do anything about it. Somehow, I would muster up enough energy to find something small and easy to get, like bugs and fruit. That little something would allow me to get something more substantial, like fish or a bird. But it never lasted long. The cycle would start over. Food came and went like the tide that stretched out before me.

For the most part, water was always available. There was one week when my source dried out for seemingly no reason and I had to resort to drinking my own urine. I attempted to make a solar still but I ended up wasting most of the urine, so I opted to chance it and drink what remained. It served no purpose, except making me sick and more dehydrated. I vowed to never drink my urine again, a vow that was easily kept. What saved me during the weeklong drought was a huge storm that rolled in. Suddenly the area went from dry to practically flooded. After the drought, I got smart about water. I save many empty coconut shells and used them to fill with water and store in case another drought happened. I even had one single turtle shell that I used as for water storage.

But of hunger and thirst, fear of the unknown was the most terrifying. Someone else was still on the island with me, and they hadn't shown themselves. It also seemed that they would go days, sometimes weeks before they came around again. It was as if they only taunted me during the times that I struggled the most, as if they enjoyed watching me suffer. I gave up on trying to make contact with them. I tried numerous times, but they always got away before I could talk to them. Whoever it was, they were always a step ahead of me.

What was weird about my fear of the other person on the island was that the fear was laced with drips of comfort. Sometimes I would talk out loud, hoping the person would hear me. I thought maybe they would eventually say something back to me. If nothing else it gave me a sense of peace to be able to talk out loud and the idea that someone could've been listening. But even with that comfort, I was deathly afraid of them. The reason they had to not communicate with me, watch me from the jungle with their stabbing eyes, and then retreat when I sought them out, was frightening. They were my only friend and my one enemy, and I had never even seen them in their entirety. It was an unusual fear. It was a lonely, comforting fear that would blanket me with sadness.

But something else was growing inside of me alongside the fear. It was deep, blunt, and heavily influential. It rooted itself in my soul and lived right under the skin. It wasn't just the fear of the other person on the island, but also the fear of never being able to leave the island. Or worse, being able to leave the island and cursing my family to go through a sort of reverse grieving process. It also stemmed from the ups and downs of survival. It weighed itself on me. It burrowed into my thoughts every day. I would sometimes shake it off, but other times I would let it grow, feed it even, and give it the life that it wanted.

Death. Death was on my mind. My own death. Suicide. How easy it would be to just end it. To just be free from all the misery, uncertainty, and tasks of trying to stay alive. It seemed that was what nature wanted anyway. It forced me to try to survive to the point where I was almost dead, then it would throw me a bone and make me start the process over again. Nature enjoys struggle. And I was more and more dancing with the idea that I would disappoint nature. Steal nature's love of struggle and replace it with death. That way I could be in control of my fate, not nature.

The thoughts of death would begin like the flicker of a light, but I would furnish that light with more power, allowing it to grow into a spotlight. A spotlight on my own death. A shining beacon of hope for the tragic adventure I placed upon myself. An end to life's adventure and a beginning to an adventure into the unknown. It was hard to fight the undertow of death's enticement. Especially when I was all alone. I knew that it was just a matter of time before I let go.

It wasn't like I hadn't tried to survive on the island. And it wasn't like I hadn't tried to leave the island. In fact, I set myself up for every possible advantage I could get. I had a huge signal fire built and ready to be lit whenever the time came, but it never did. It stood a few yards away from my beach camp, with an almost sad, tired shape. As if it had been set up for too long and it knew that it would never be lit. Its destiny never fulfilled.

I had tried my hand at building a small raft and heading out into the ocean. I hoped that maybe I could drift somewhere populated, or that maybe I would be found by a passing vessel. But after building the boat and putting it in the water, it immediately fell apart. However, I didn't give up. The next boat didn't fall apart, but a huge storm swelled up and threw me and my steady boat back to the island. It felt that maybe the island didn't want me to leave. Like maybe my destiny was to be on the island. To live and die on the island. My adventure was to be my opus.

Each time I tried to escape, the island held me tightly and wouldn't release. Each time I fashioned a way to let the world know I was there, no one saw. I was doomed to spend the rest of my life on the island. I just wasn't sure I was going to let the island dictate how long that would be. I was the master of my fate, and nothing else could determine when I would take my last breath, except myself.

Although the idea of death laced its way through my brain, I still had the underlying humanistic need to survive. I still ate, I still drank, but more importantly, I still fought the thoughts of death. Even though there was a huge voice in my head churning the wheel of my own demise, I was still there to put the brakes on it until I was ready for it.

Honestly, I didn't want to die. I simply wanted end my time on Nightmare Island and go back to my family. But I knew that it wasn't as cut and dry as it sounded. Sometimes I would take trips up to the top of the cape, stand on the edge, and visualize falling. It would be quick, practically painless, and most of all, intrinsically beautiful. There would be times that I would stand at the top of the cape for hours, visualizing it so deeply that I would think that the jump had already happened. I would only realize that I was still standing on the cape when I would open my eyes. I would lose my balance for a moment and almost fall off. I would then climb down and continue my life of surviving as if nothing happened. It was almost like there were two people in my head. The one that continued to survive and the one that wanted nothing more than to just take a step off the cape and end it all. The latter of the two was winning the battle more and more. Death seemed like the logical thing to do.

Don't get me wrong, I cherished life as much as the next person. But, something inside of me wanted finality. Something in me wanted the struggle to end. I knew that my death would bring me peace. But there were two sides to the argument. One voice would scream to take the leap off the cape and end the pain and daily strife of island existence. But the other voice would jump right in and say that help was right around the corner. The voices would argue back and forth, not giving me time to hear them in their entirety. The arguments were so frequent and without antecedents that I began to wonder if they were my own thoughts or the thoughts of someone losing their grip on reality.

CHAPTER
THIRTEEN

It was beautiful. The deep azure sky, ribboned with creamy white clouds, penetrated my eyes. The sun was just beginning to set, and on the horizon a multitude of yellows, oranges, pinks, and purples grew in intensity with every passing moment. Far below the cape I could hear the static-like sound of the waves as they impacted the cape head. I could see the froth that would churn up and fizzle out on the rocks. It was gorgeous. I drank it all in. The perfect ending.

It had been three months since the arguments in my head began, and after more pain, struggle, and waiting for rescue, the voice that shouted death had silenced its opposition. No more did I guess at which voice to listen to. No more did I wonder what tomorrow would bring. I wouldn't be here to see anymore tomorrows. No longer would I battle the pain and the unknown. I wouldn't know uncertainty anymore. It would end for me, and I was at peace with the idea of such a conclusion.

The wind was gentle and at my back. It was almost as if it was ushering me to complete my final task. How simple it would be. The difference between existing or not was as easy as an effortless step off a rock. It amazed me how fragile life can be. How one small action can alter things in a way that's larger than the sum of its parts. Something so minuscule like not having enough water can lead to the end of a life. Or how a small mistake like drifting into another lane while driving, even if that mistake is only measured in mere inches, can alter the lives of many. Not just the car or cars involved. But the families of the people in the cars. Or the people that show up to the scene of the accident. The stress of seeing potential horror. It rippled all the way around.

My ripple would be less significant, however. I knew this and it affected me little. I had been on the island so long that I was sure that my family has already mourned me and, with any luck, moved on. Any search and rescue parties would have long since ended their quest. I existed only on the island. I was only a memory, a sad thought, a picture on the mantle that was too difficult to look at. I assumed that somewhere in the world I had a headstone. I already had my funeral. My family and friends now knew me as deceased. By ending everything on the island I was only bringing their knowledge to its inevitable completion.

It has been said that when one is about to die their entire life flashes before them. I wondered when that moment would take place. Would it be right as I step off the cape? Or would it be after I landed on the jagged rocks below, moments before my heart ceases to pound in my chest? Maybe it would never happen. Maybe I wouldn't get the pleasure of being able to see every moment of my

110

life flash before me. That thought was sad enough to allow but a single tear to escape from my eye. I wiped it away and stared deeply at the growing sunset. In all reality, I didn't want a recap of my life. Or, rather, I didn't want a recap of my life on Nightmare Island. Living through it once was plenty enough. To have had to go through it again, however brief, would've be torturous.

"God," I said. "I know I haven't spoken to you in a long time. And I am sure you probably think of me as someone who doesn't believe in you." I paused and felt the wind blow through my hair, almost as if God was assuring me that he was listening. "But I do believe in you," I continued. "Not just in this moment. But deep down I have always known that you are there, helping and guiding me in a way I could never understand. I don't exactly know what the rule is on taking your own life, but from what I've gathered over the years, it's the ultimate sin. It's unforgivable. If this is true, then my words are meaningless. But I beg of you to forgive me. I beg that you understand why it is that I am doing this." Another warm breeze blew across my face, like the soft caress of a comforting palm. "I hope that you do."

It was not normal for me to ask God of anything. It seemed that God was never there for me in the past. Generally, when I would pray, if at all, it was only in my head. But this was the last call. My one final plea before I took the plunge to the sharpness below. The wind changed directions and slammed into my front. It was stronger than the gentle breeze that was embracing my back and face. I thought that maybe it was God trying to tell me to turn around and reconsider. But it was too late for me.

Next to where I was standing was a small rock that jolted out of the cape and had a sort of flat surface. It was conspicuous and perfect for my last words. I kneeled down, and with my knife, scribed my epitaph:

Damon G.
A true adventure awaits me now…

I was ready to do the deed. To end the meaningless struggle that Nightmare Island gifted me. My eyes instinctively closed. I drew in a deep breath of the warm tropical air. My last breath. It was sweet and wonderfully fulfilling. My right foot lifted up and my body leaned toward the abyss. I could feel gravity pulling me down as I angled further. My mind was blank, peaceful, and accepting of my fate.

"No, wait," a voice from behind me screamed.

CHAPTER FOURTEEN

I felt my body heave around, doing a 180 degree turn back toward the cliff's edge. This sudden movement, coupled with the crumbling rocks, made me slip. I lost my footing and felt myself falling. That's what I wanted after all. I wanted to fall. I wanted to die. To end the bitter fight for survival on Nightmare Island. The fall was short. I had somehow managed to catch myself on the rocks and a few plants that grew. My heart was racing. I was dangling off the edge of the cliff. But why? I could not figure out why I had not completed the jump. My memory was too full of adrenaline to remember what had happened. I wondered if I had second thoughts. My grip on the plants and rocks was firm, but the plants roots were shallow and beginning to pull up from the earth. I used all of my strength to try and pull myself up. That was when I felt it. A hand. A human hand. It grasped onto my hand and pulled me back onto the top of the cliff. I laid on the ground looking up at the shape that was standing above me. My vision was blurry from the dust that was stirred up and all I could make out was a rough human shape.

"What the hell just happened," I said aloud. The form began to focus into that of a female. Her hair was long and brown and she had a worried look on her face. Her eyes were large and luminous. Penetratingly green eyes just stared at me. "Who are you?"

"I'm glad I made it in time," she said. "You were standing up here for a long time. I knew something wasn't right." Her voice was soft and her words skipped off her lips like rocks on a lake.

I stood and brushed myself off, clouds of dust wafted into the wind and disappeared into the space between the earth and the sky. I was silent and just stood there staring at her. She did the same. I was a bit taller than her, but she was not short by any means. After a moment we both had caught our breath and could stand still without heaving up and down from lack of oxygen.

"Who are you?" I asked. "You almost killed me." The words came out of my mouth rudely and without truth.

"I almost killed you?" She said defensively. "You were clearly going to jump off the cliff. If anything, I saved your life." Her soft tone quickly changed into a more angered one.

"I didn't ask for your help," I said. "I was perfectly content with what I was doing." She glared at me in a way that I forgot was possible. "So who are you and what are you doing here?"

"I don't know," she simply said.

"What do you mean you don't know?" I replied. "You can't just show up and not tell me who you are and what it is you're doing here."

"I mean I don't know," she said. She turned around and began to walk down the cape path.

"Wait, where are you going? So you're not going to even tell me who you are, or how you got here, or why the hell you decided to pop out at the worst possible time?" I said following her.

She stopped in the middle of the path. "Just follow me. We should probably get something to eat and I saw that you had some food at your camp," she said.

"Wait," I said stopping in my tracks, stunned at the sudden revelation that came over me. "You're the one that's been stalking me. You're the one that's been taunting me from the jungle, aren't you?"

"Just shut up and follow me. We can talk about this later," she said sternly. She kept walking but I stayed still for a moment. I was stunned for numerous reasons. My mind was in overdrive. I should've been dead, not arguing with some random person. But I followed her nonetheless, more out of curiosity than anything else.

When we both got to my camp there was a weird aura that surrounded it. It was like the camp knew that I should not have returned. I knew that I wasn't supposed to still be around. I should've been dead, but there I was, standing next to the place I had lived for so long.

"So, I want to know what your name is." I said.

"I told you," she replied. "I don't know."

"What do you mean?" I asked. "How do you not know your own name? Is this just another one of your weird ways to screw with me?"

"I don't know my name. I think I have amnesia or something," she said. "And I wasn't screwing with you. I was keeping my distance."

"Amnesia? I'm sorry, I'm very confused right now," I replied, perplexed at the situation.

"You and me both," she immediately replied. "I don't remember who I am, how I got here, how long I've been here, or anything. All I know is I woke up on a beach on the other side of the island with a very sore head and no memory of anything."

"That's weird," I said.

"You're telling me," she said. There was a long pause as she started messing around with the fire pit. "I'll start the fire if you go down and grab the fish you caught."

"How do you know about the fish I caught?" I said.

"Like you said earlier, I'm the one who has been stalking you," she said. She spoke of stalking me in a funny, joking, and playful way, as if stalking someone on a deserted island isn't weird or creepy. I just scowled at her and headed down to get the fish.

There was something numbing about existing. After all, cleaning the guts out of two ocean fish was not something I intended to be doing. But there I was, doing it. It was surreal. It was like I cheated death. Or maybe God heard my prayers and made this person reveal themselves to save me. Regardless, I felt ghostly. Like I shouldn't be here. But as I ripped the insides out of a small sea creature, I looked at this random person blowing life into the fire. It made me realize that maybe death was not my fate, but rather, maybe my fate was to survive and this person was the catalyst to that survival.

"Here's the fish," I said.

"Excellent. I just got the fire going good enough to cook with," she said. She was entrancing. She manipulated the fire like it a part of her. She would whisper with air and it would respond with fire. Almost as if they were one in the same. She tossed the fish into the drum and set it aside. "Let me use your knife real quick," she said. I handed it to her and she grabbed a coconut that I had previously husked and gave it a hard smack with the back of the knife. She repeated this until the coconut broke in two. She carefully poured the sweet milk into the drum with the fish and set the drum on the fire.

"You seem to be very good at all this," I said. "How long have you been here again?"

"Well, I don't know exactly," she said. "But from what I can figure I have been here for almost a year, maybe more."

"I think that's about how long I've been here, too," I said. She gave the pot a stir with the knife. "Why did you hide from me? Why didn't you help me when I asked for it?"

"I didn't know what you were capable of," she simply said. I understood what she meant. If I was alone, didn't know who I was, and saw a random person I probably wouldn't let them know I existed either. But it wasn't enough of an excuse.

"Then why did you watch me so much?" I asked. "I mean, it seemed like you were following me, taunting me even. You watched me suffer. You saw me and yet you did nothing to help me."

"You were the only thing that kept me sane and alive," she replied stirring the fish again.

"What do you mean?" I asked confused.

"When I woke up on the beach I was alone, scared, and had no idea what I was doing," she said. "I figured there would be a town or something somewhere on the island so I went searching. I found you instead. I watched you figure things out. Fire, water, food, shelter, everything. I just copied you. I watched you because I wanted to learn, or rather, I needed to learn. But I found myself coming back to just watch you."

"Why?" I asked.

"I don't know. I guess you were a comfort to me," she said shyly. "Even though I was scared to actually show myself to you, it was nice to know that there was someone else here with me, experiencing the

117

same turmoil I was. I mean, I was afraid of you at the same time. I didn't know how you would react when you saw me."

"I felt the opposite," I said.

"Why?" She asked.

"Well, I didn't know who you were. As far as I knew you were a murderer. Honestly, you scared me so much that I almost jumped off a cliff today. I mean, it wasn't only you, but between trying to just survive and then have someone messing with you for so long, I just couldn't do it anymore. I couldn't sleep well knowing that there was someone out there watching me, but didn't care enough to help." I said.

She took a deep breath, "I'm sorry."

"Thank you," I said. "I just wished you would've showed yourself sooner. I forgot what it was like to talk to someone, well, besides myself."

"Yeah, I enjoyed listening to you talk to yourself," she said with a smile.

"It was the only thing I could do to keep myself from going nuts," I said.

"The fish is almost done," she said giving it another stir.

"So, what can I call you?" I asked.

"What do you mean?" She said.

"Well, if you can't remember your name I need something to call you," I said.

"Well, it's not like there's a bunch of people here to get me confused with," she said smiling. A laugh escaped my mouth. It wasn't intentional, but rather, it slipped out after so long without anything funny. It was sort of strange to feel emotions and feelings that I hadn't felt in so long.

"I guess that's true," I said with a chuckle. "But, you should still have a name."

"I don't know," she said thinking. "Just call me whatever you want."

"Okay," I said considering the options. "Wow. I've never had to name someone before." My mind drew a blank.

"Well, don't think too hard," she said.

"Oh, I've got it," I said realizing the perfect name. "I'll name you after one of my favorite movies. It should be easy enough to remember."

"Okay, what is it?" She said wearily.

"Willow," I said. "I will call you Willow."

"What movie is that from?" She asked.

"The movie is called Willow," I said. "Haven't you seen it?"

"I don't remember seeing it, but I don't remember much," she replied.

"Then it's settled. Your name will be Willow from here on out," I said stamping the air with an imaginary seal.

"Okay, so what's your name?" Willow asked.

"I'm Damon," I replied.

"Nice to meet you, Damon," Willow said. "Wish it was under better circumstances."

"Agreed," I replied. "Listen, about what you saw on the cliff…"

"Hey, forget about it," she interrupted. "I won't mention it if you don't mention it."

"Deal," I said with a hint of embarrassment in my voice.

She carefully moved the drum that contained the fish and coconut milk away from the fire and gave it a final stir. She waved her hand in the steam, wafting the aroma into her nose.

"Mmm," she said pleasantly. "Now that smells good."

"You're telling me," I said. "Let's eat."

It wasn't long before the sun was set and our bellies were full. We both sat in silence for a while, enjoying the view and relishing in the good meal. It was probably the first time I truly enjoyed the island. Something as simple as another person made the sun setting seem more brilliant, the stars more like diamonds glistening in the sky, and the lap of the ocean like a beautiful sonata. It was as if all my loneliness left me all at once. I was no longer scared of the unknown, the uncertainties, or the struggle. Something about sharing those things made them easier to bear.

"That was delicious," I said breaking the silence.

"Thank you," she said.

"So tell me about yourself," I stupidly asked. "Well, I mean, I know you can't remember anything, but like, tell me who you are now, since you woke up on the beach. What have you been up to? Besides stalking me."

"It's been weird," Willow said. "Waking up on a beach with no one around or nothing in sight is scary. I was afraid. I'm pretty sure I spent like an hour just yelling help into the air. I didn't know what to do. I just stayed on the beach for like three days. By the third day I realized that no one was coming, so I decided I would head into the island to search for a town or something. I was smart though, like you. I made the word help out of branches in case someone came while I was in the jungle."

"That is smart," I said. "You practically did exactly what I did."

"Well, the jungle was not a friendly place," Willow said with a pause. "It's cramped, always wet, filled with horrible bugs that just want to bite, and none of the water is safe to drink."

"I take it you found that out the hard way?" I asked.

"Yeah, after several hours without water I didn't think about what jungle water could do to me," she said. "I found a small puddle of water and just drank it dry. It wasn't long before I was, well, you know."

"Yeah, that sucks," I said. "So what did you do? I mean, how did you survive without clean water and food?"

"I mainly ate bugs, small lizards, and fruits that looked familiar," she said. "Weird how I can't remember my name but I can remember what a mango looks like. As far as water goes, I would heat up rocks in a fire and drop them into a coconut filled with water. Enough rocks and the water boils. Not sure how safe it is, but I didn't have any problems with my insides after that. And as you know, you make friends with coconuts real quick."

"Dang," I said amazed. "I never thought about the rock idea. I read about that in a survival book but the idea never even crossed my mind. I am seriously disappointed in myself."

She chuckled slightly and then said, "I have no idea how I knew to do that. It just popped into my head."

"I've had a few of those moments before. Sometimes you know more than you even realize," I said. "The brain can be a really powerful thing."

"Yeah, it can. Well, I think we should get some rest," Willow said stretching. "Tomorrow we should figure out what we're going to do."

"What do you mean?" I asked.

"Well, if we're going to be in this together we're going to need a bigger shelter, more food, more water, the whole works," she said. I instantly felt stupid. I didn't even think about the issues of surviving with two people. It's double everything. It wouldn't be hard, but certain things would just need an upgrade. I would've thought of that but I was too enthralled with her story, the beauty around me, and my full stomach to realize it.

"Yeah, you're right," I said. "You can sleep inside the shelter tonight and we'll build a bigger one tomorrow. I'll sleep out here."

"Are you sure?" She asked.

"Yeah, it's beautiful out here," I said. I laid my head back onto my hands and peered at the great unknown in the sky.

"Goodnight, Damon," she said.

"Goodnight, Willow," I said.

CHAPTER
FIFTEEN

The smell of breakfast filled my dreams and gave me a nostalgic feeling of being back at home. I dreamed my mother was making bacon, eggs, and a nice stack of her Norwegian pancakes, lusciously smothered in butter and syrup. It seemed so real, so lifelike, that I thought I could hear the popping of bacon fat as it rendered in a pan. The popping felt like it was growing louder in my dream. So loud that I began to awake from the dream. But the popping didn't cease. It continued just as loud. As I stretched, my nose drew in a breath of fried eggs and bacon. My eyes, still adjusting to the brightness of the tropics, searched for the source.

"About time you wake up," Willow said using my knife to stir the drum. What she stirred sizzled away wonderfully. I was intrigued.

"What do you have?" I asked. "It smells amazing."

"You aren't going to believe this," she said. "But, we're having scrambled eggs and bacon for breakfast, with a side of fresh fruit." I was shocked. Surely I was still dreaming. How on earth would she have acquired bacon and eggs? It's not like there was a grocery store nearby.

I quickly stood from my makeshift beach bed and rushed over to her. "What the hell?" I said amazed at what I saw. In the pan was indeed a pile of soft, yellowy eggs, scrambling away before my eyes. What was even more amazing was what was next to the pan in the fire. A small pig. Its skin was golden brown and it was weeping delicious grease from anywhere the flames licked at it. A delightful sizzle filled my ears and the smell almost brought me to my knees. It was a salty, savory, and decadent sight to behold.

"I hope you're hungry," Willow said before I could get a word in.

"How...? How...?" Was all I could say. I stood dumbfounded for a moment before I burst into a sort of shouting fit that is usually reserved only for sports fans when their teams win a big championship. Willow looked at me with a sweet grin, both proud of what she had accomplished, and excited by my reaction. "How did this happen?" I asked.

"Well, while you were snoozing the day away, I went out to look for something to eat," she said. "I really only expected to find some coconuts or mangoes, but I came across a bird nest on the ground instead. It must've fallen out of the tree or something. There were five eggs in it, each one a little smaller than a chicken egg."

"I can't believe it," I said amazed at her luck.

"I know. So, on the way back I found some mangoes and a coconut to go along with it," she said. "I figured that would be a pretty good breakfast."

"How in the hell did you get a pig?" I asked.

"I just heard some snorting sounds," she said. "I tracked them down and there was a mother pig and three piglets. I had your knife still and thought I'd try to catch one. After setting the fruit and eggs down I slowly stalked one of the piglets. I had to stop in my tracks because one practically came right up to me. I mean, it was within one or two feet."

"Oh, my gosh," I said completely enthralled in her story. "What did you do?"

"I waited until it turned back around and I grabbed it," she said making a grabbing motion with her hands. "It squirmed and shook and squealed so loudly it startled me and I almost dropped it. Thankfully the mother and the other two piglets ran off. I bet they were frightened as well."

"So how did you, you know?" I asked.

"I tucked it under my arms and used the knife right under its chin," she said miming the motions. "It made a horrible gurgling sound, shook violently, and then stopped."

Using a stick and the knife she flipped the piglet to cook the other side. A loud, wonderful sizzle filled the air as the fire got doused with new fat. A plume of beautiful smoke wafted into the air, followed by a burst of flames as the liquid fat ignited. I waved the smoke into my face and inhaled the briny aroma. The side of the piglet that was revealed was amazingly brown, crisp, and oozing warm liquid fat. My mouth watered and I could feel goosebumps forming on my body.

"I am honestly speechless," I said. Willow beamed proudly. She knew what she had done and she could see in my eyes how amazed I was at such an accomplishment.

Our eyes met, both knowing what was coming next. It would be something sinful, nefarious, and maybe even criminal. Either way, it would be a euphoric experience that would leave us breathless and begging for more.

"Let's eat," Willow said as she removed the fluffy scramble from the fire.

"Oh, my gosh, I am so ready for this," I said rubbing my hands together in excitement. "Wait a second. You caught the pig, killed the pig, and even gutted it?"

"Yeah, that part wasn't fun," she said squishing her face together in disgust. "Next time, that'll be your job." We both laughed, high on the notion that a good meal was on its way.

"Oh, please let there be many next times," I said salivating. "I could get used to this."

She carefully removed the pig from the fire and placed it onto a couple of palm fronds. The grease still sputtered away on the skin of the pig like a twinkling night sky, the running grease like shooting stars. "Do the honors?" She asked.

"I couldn't possibly," I said. "You rocked it and deserve to be the one that carves into that beauty."

"I insist," she said with a wink.

"Okay," I said taking the knife from her. The piglet wasn't very big. It was probably quite young, maybe two or so weeks old. It weighed about four to six pounds, most of that bone and fat. But there was still quite a lot of meat. More than I had seen in a long time. Most of the meat I was use to eating on the island was of the ocean variety. I was ecstatic. I began to carve into the pig. The skin was crispy, sealing in the majority of the juices, and it cracked when the knife sliced into it. A rush of aromatic steam released into the air. The steam had not only helped cook the pig, but also kept the meat

126

amazingly succulent. A puddle of wonderful fatty juices gathered on the palm fronds. For a brief moment I caught the reflection of myself smiling in the gathering juices.

I took a couple palm fronds that Willow nicely laid out as plates and put a heap of meat on each of them. I handed the knife to Willow and she used it to scoop out the eggs. She graciously gave me far more than half the eggs.

"You don't have to do that," I said stopping her. "We can split it evenly. I mean, technically you found them. Realistically, you should have more."

"I want you to have more," she said. "It's my gift to you." She grinned and continued piling more eggs onto my frond. "After all, I was kind of weird. The whole stalking thing, as you put it, was strange. This is my way of saying I'm sorry."

"Thank you," I said gratefully. "Apology accepted."

After Willow placed some eggs on her plate she cut up some mango and divided it between us. Laid out before us was two heaping piles of food. Our eyes were probably bigger than our stomachs, but we didn't care. We were going to eat like royalty, and quite possibly, to the point of sickness. It was Thanksgiving on Nightmare Island and we were ready to unbutton our pants.

"This is so good," I said shoveling a mass of pork into my mouth. Juices dripped from the corners of my mouth.

"You got a little something," she said pointing at my mouth.

"What?" I said chewing my food like a cow chews its cud.

"Here, let me," she said. She used her shirt and wiped the grease from my face. There was something sensual about the way in which she did it. Slow, precise, and all the while staring into my eyes. I wasn't sure what to do, so I just stared back into her pine-green eyes, slightly uncomfortable, slightly grateful. Not just grateful that she cleaned my face, but grateful there was another person with me. Something as simple as the touch of another human, even though the fibers of a cotton shirt, was enough to ease my mind and give me a sense of purpose. When she finished wiping my face she let out an adorable chuckle. I followed with a nervous laugh, realizing I had been making awkward eye contact the entire time.

"Thanks," I said.

"No problem," she replied.

Willow was a neat eater. While she easily put down a huge pile of food, she somehow managed to do it with graceful deportment. She would take small, thoughtful bites, carefully chewing and savoring every piece. This was a stark contrast to myself. I would stuff a mound of food into my gullet, chewing only enough to allow a swallow to take effect. I wasn't normally a messy eater, it was just after I lived on fish, bugs, and fruit for months, I was overly enthusiastic about eggs and pork.

"Ugh, I am so full," I said rubbing my stomach. Both of our lips and fingers were glossy with pig fat and we wore the grease like a badge of honor.

"Me too," Willow said. "I haven't been this full since, well, since I can remember."

We both sat, enjoying our full bellies, watching the ocean churn, and for once, taking pleasure in the company of another person. The sun was high, warm, but not uncomfortably hot. A gentle breeze swayed the tall jungle trees and cooled our skin.

"What do you want to do today?" I asked.

"Umm..." she mumbled, contorting her face while trying to think of something.

"We should probably build a bigger shelter," I suggested.

"That's a good idea," she said. "You know, there's a spot in this meadow that I have used for shelter. It's got big sheets of metal in it. Sometimes, if I was in the area, I would stay under them when it rained."

"Like plane pieces?" I asked, slightly disturbed to even utter such a question.

"Yeah, I guess," she said, seeming not fully sure of her answer. "I mean, it almost looks more like the roof of a house. Like one of those tin roof houses you'd see along a coastline. But, I guess it could be pieces of a plane."

"That's weird if it's pieces of a house," I said curiously.

"Why?" She asked.

"Well, there's no houses on this island," I said. "Although, I guess someone could've either lived here a long time ago or they could've brought it here to use as a makeshift shelter."

"I bet it's for hunting," she said. "I bet someone brought it here and used it as a hunting blind or something." Her surmise impressed me.

"You know, I bet you're right about that," I said nodding my head in approval. "I could imagine a lot of people hunting here. I've seen lots of different animals here. Heck, there's even pigs." I paused and thought for a moment. "Let's do it. That metal would go a long way to protect us from storms and such."

"Then it's settled," she said standing up. "We will venture into the heart of the jungle and retrieve the sheets of metal." She placed her fists onto her hips like a superhero standing at attention. I let out a slight giggle and she responded with a smile that revealed a beautiful set of milky white teeth.

We stopped at the water hole to fill up the water bottle for our trip in the jungle. She had guessed that the spot with the sheets of metal was closer to the other side of the island, an area that I had not been before.

"You know, this is about the spot that we chased each other around many months ago," I said dipping the plastic bottle into the oversized puddle of water. "That was a terrible day for me."

"Yeah, sorry about that," Willow said looking embarrassed.

"Why were you following me that day?" I asked.

"I don't know," she said bringing her thick brown eyebrows down. "I had been scared of you for so long that I figured I could try scaring you away from me. Stupid, I know."

"Besides that hardly making any sense, it pretty much worked," I said capping the bottle. "I hid from you and when you got ahead of me I tried to catch you. If I had, I wouldn't have known what to do. I was so angry, scared, and confused. Just the thought of someone taunting me for so long made me mad."

"Yeah, I'm sorry about that," she said looking down at the ground ashamed.

"I ended up falling down a pretty steep hill," I said with a chuckle. "You are a fast runner, I'll give you that."

"Thank you," she said with a sort of cute smugness. "Hey, are you going to boil that water before we drink it?"

"Dang it," I said. "I hadn't thought about that. We'll keep it just in case. I guess it'd be better to have stomach issues than be dehydrated."

"True," she said.

Willow led the way through the thick jungle. At times, it seemed as if we were going in circles, but I trusted that she knew where she was going. The jungle seemed alive with sounds and smells that I had rarely noticed before. Weird unseen creatures squeaked and chirped all around us. The moment we would get near a creature it would scurry off into the thick distance, rustling leaves along the way. The musky smell of humid plants filled the air, almost choking out any hope of fresh oxygen. The humidity clung to our skin like a leech and wouldn't let up. The jungle was not going to be easy for us to walk through. There was no path, no trail that allowed for constant travel. Instead, it was the huge task of slashing foliage with a knife, ripping plants out of the way with bare hands, and many times, dancing over large thatches of decaying debris. It zapped the energy and spirit right out of us, but we continued.

"It's shouldn't be too far from here," Willow said. Her words were refreshing. Rest was needed, for both of us. Our clothes dripped with a crude mixture of sweat, dew, plant juice, and other unknown liquid substances.

Reprieve was soon found, as the jungle opened up into a vast meadow dotted with small pools of limpid water. A shallow stream snaked its way through the meadow, touching each one of the small pools before disappearing into the darkness of the thick wilderness. A cool breeze blanketed itself over my skin like a sort of natural air conditioning. Willow sprung to life and began running off toward the closest pool of water. She had a childlike bounce to her step that made me beam before I too pounced off toward the same pool.

"I'm going in," she said standing at the edge of the water. She began taking off her shoes and I followed suit.

"This is going to be so amazing," I said hopping on one foot as I tried to get my shoe off. Willow began taking her clothes off, first the shirt, then her pants. Before I knew it she was standing in front of me in nothing but her underwear. Her skin was like ivory, slowly fading into a dark brown tan where her clothes did not cover. The sweat on her body glistened in the sun as she moved. Her underwear clung to her tightly and left almost nothing to the imagination. I realized I was staring and quickly looked down at the water.

"Are you going to swim in your clothes?" She asked with a snicker. I stumbled to find words. I had been alone on the island for so long I forgot what beauty a woman's body emanates. I peered toward her and stole another look, feeling guilty I had done so. But, she was as beautiful as an island sunset, graceful as a swaying palm, and as enchanting as the clear night sky. All the time spent hating whoever it was in the jungle that stalked me seemed to slip away as I took quick looks at her frame. I could feel my body reacting in a way that would be quite embarrassing, so I shook the thoughts away.

"Of course not," I said sheepishly. I began to peel the clothes away from my sticky skin, leaving only my boxers on. It felt good once I was free of the clothes, but I was instantly embarrassed to find that Willow was staring at me with wide eyes. It was kind of satisfying knowing that I wasn't alone in the curious gazes. She looked away from me and without any warning hurled herself into the pool of water, making a large splash as she entered.

"Oh, yes," she said as she surfaced from under the water. "It's absolutely wonderful. Are you coming in or are you just going to stand there all day?"

As I had in my youth, I yelled, "cannonball," and flung myself into the pool. "Whew," I said. "That is wonderful." I wiped my eyes clear of water and when they opened Willow was wading right in front of me. It was kind of a shock. She was just looking at me.

"You splashed me," she said in a serious tone.

"I'm sorry," I said, figuring I must've offended her in some way.

"It's okay," she said now with a sweet tone. "But now, you will feel my wrath." Her arm skimmed the surface of the water, bringing with it a wave of the cool liquid hurtling at my face. It collided with a force I would not have expected from someone with such a gentle demeanor.

"Oh, it's on," I said wiping the water from my eyes. Willow had begun swimming away from me, all the while using her feet to splatter the water in my direction. I returned fire as I swam toward her, showering her with huge showers of water. I reached her before she could retaliate and sent a monsoon of a wave careening toward her head. It engulfed her and she let out a laugh while trying to splash me back. She continued to splash at me but I swam around silently behind her. I made no noise. Once she ceased her splashing she looked around for me. She turned around to find me almost nose to nose with her. A single gasp released itself from her ruby lips.

"Gosh you scared me," she said.

"Then I succeeded," I replied cockily. We both laughed, but then, once the laughing ceased, we just stared at each other. Not a normal stare. It was a deep stare. The kind of stare before a kiss. Our heads moved in close, our eyes closed, it was going to happen. I was going to kiss her, and she was going to kiss me.

An instantaneous crack of thunder interrupted. The sound was fierce and jolted Willow and I apart from each other. We both looked off into the distance, toward the part of the jungle that we came from. A gloomy black cloud loomed over the jungle canopy. It was moving fast, and right toward us with a fury.

"Oh, crap," I said. "It's coming right at us."

"That does not look good," Willow said. "We need get out of here right now." Without hesitance both Willow and I got out of the pool and put our clothes on as quickly as one could being soaked with water. "Where are we going to go?"

I looked around and saw an area that wasn't too far away and seemed to have a decent amount of cover. It was at the jungle fringe and was in the opposite direction of the storm.

"Over there," I said pointing. "We need to hurry and take cover."

We both bolted into a hurried sprint toward the jungle edge. The storm followed us closely and sent deafening crashes of thunder and flashes of lightning behind us. We hurdled over rocks and plants with no problem and soon found ourselves under the cover of many trees and plants. We barely had time to situate ourselves when we were caught up in the storm. A deluge of rain poured onto the trees and plants above us, making its way down to us, and soaking us to the bone. The water was unusually warm for the tropics. The sound of thunder echoed all around us and did not cease for even a slight moment. I could've screamed into Willow's ear and she would not have been able to hear a single word.

I took my button-up shirt and tried to wrap it around Willow, bringing her in close to me and offering both myself and her some comfort. We would have to brave whatever the storm brought.

I prayed the storm would be short-lived. But there was a part of me that enjoyed the embrace we shared during the tempest. There was a sort of closeness that I had lacked being alone for so long. It was a wonderful experience, even if the storm tried to diminish any of its grandeur.

During all the commotion, my mind wandered to the moment where we almost kissed. I imagined what it would've been like in great detail in my mind. Her crimson lips, full and soft. My hand caressing her silken nape as the kiss became more passionate. And the moment where the kiss ended and we both looked deeply into each other's eyes, realizing at once that we would no longer be alone on Nightmare Island, but rather, together, with someone.

I wondered if her thoughts were the same as mine.

CHAPTER SIXTEEN

The storm raged on for what seemed like forever. But I didn't mind. Both Willow and I sat under the cover of the jungle, and while it offered little protection from the elements, we had each other in that moment. It was something that I hadn't had in a long time. I weathered many storms before Willow, but the companionship made it more than bearable. In fact, I enjoyed her presence.

Lightning burst from the sky and collided with the ground, sometimes hardly more than several yards away from us. The sound ricocheted within the forest, pulsing past our eardrums and into the thicket. Even with all the rain, I could see the surrounding grass ignite from the explosion of energy the lightning released. It was quickly put out by the rain. At times, Willow and I would randomly lift our heads up, with mouths agape, and take in a drink of the fresh rainwater. We were, undoubtedly, hydrated both inside and out.

The sun peered out from behind the clouds and shone brightly onto the soaked ground and trees around us. The storm raged on, but it had passed over us and we were left in awe of its might. The trees and plants dripped onto us as we stood and walked to the meadow and jungle fringe to stretch and recuperate.

"Wow," I said. "That was crazy."

"You're not kidding," Willow said trying to squeeze out water from her clothes. "I've never seen a storm like that. It was angry and violent. I will admit, I was a little scared."

"I wasn't," I said lying through my teeth. The truth was, I was scared. But that feeling was squelched by the comfort of being so close to Willow.

"Really, you weren't scared?" She asked in amazement.

"No, not really," I said. "It was actually kind of cool when you think about it."

"I guess," Willow said brushing off my egotism. "We'd better get a move on, that cost us a lot of daylight. My guess is we're going to be spending the night in the jungle."

"Yeah, that should be fun," I said sarcastically. "We should fill up the water bottle before we go back into the jungle." I dumped the jungle water out and put the bottle under a leaf that had a stream of rainwater still running off of it. It quickly filled the bottle.

Willow took a moment to get her bearings and off she went, myself quickly behind her. We trudged through the jungle at the speed of a swift snail. All in all, we were silent, with the occasional grunt as a vine tripped one of us up, breaking through the awkwardness like a machete through a ripe mango.

The part of the tangled wasteland we were in was different than any other part I had been in before. There was an unusual smell about the place. Floral, yet rotten, musky, and quite nauseating. It was hard to pinpoint what the smell was, but I figured it was a mix of decaying plants and animals, fragrant flowers, and the recent rain mixing it all together like a bad perfume.

Weird thoughts danced around my mind as we traversed the foliage. I had almost ended my life. I had given up on trying to survive. But, there I was, walking in some foreign jungle with a beautiful woman that gave me comfort. I knew that in the grand scheme we had just met, but there was something about another human that made life worth it. It made me want to push on, do better, and beat this eclectic challenge that life had dealt me.

"We should take a rest," Willow said. Her voice startled me out of my mind. "Drink some water and then move on." I handed her the water bottle.

"Listen, about what happened at the pool back there," I began. Willow quickly interrupted.

"Look, don't worry about it," she said. "We were both caught up in the moment and almost did something stupid. Let's just forget about it and move on." She took a big swill from the bottle. My heart dropped. I was going to tell her that I wished it had happened. That I understood that it may have been premature, but there was something between us that couldn't be denied. Her denial of the event, or any future events, kind of startled me. I figured she would've been on the same page that I was on.

She gave the bottle of water back to me and I took a big drink, drowning away and masking any visual inflictions I may have gave away on my face.

"Okay," I said. "We'll just pretend it never happened." The words were bitter and I instantly regretted saying them. I should've shouted that we should pursue each other, but I didn't. I simply gave in.

"Let's get a move on," Willow said.

We hiked for another few hours, and by this time the daylight waned considerably. It was possible to see scatters of daylight above us, but the thick jungle didn't allow very much to penetrate the interior. After some deliberation we both decided that we would make a small camp for the night and continue our journey the next morning.

"Tomorrow we have to tackle that hill," Willow said. "We have to go up and over it and then hike a little more before we get to the spot where the metal sheets are at." She pointed to a large and steep hill that jutted out of the ground and shot toward the sky. It may as well have been a mountain. The brush seemed so thick that it was impossible to see the top from where we were.

Willow gathered large branches for a quick lean-to shelter and I gathered wood for a fire. She had thankfully packed a small amount of leftover pork for us to eat. If she hadn't, we would've been without food for the night, and after the amount of hiking we completed, this would've been quite draining on our energy stores.

After some work we had a small shelter that had just enough room for both of us. We also had a pretty decent fire roaring along. We shoved chunks of pork onto some sticks we found and roasted them over the fire. Fat dripped onto the embers and made a delightful sizzle. The smell filled the air and slightly masked the horrendous smell that plagued us. Although, at that point, we were mostly used to its pungent aroma.

140

"I'm still amazed that you caught a pig," I said rotating my skewer of pork over the fire.

"Why? Because I'm a girl?" Willow asked teasingly.

"No, of course not," I said. "It's just impressive, that's all. I mean, I never caught a pig. I could barely get fish." Willow beamed from ear to ear, obviously proud of her accomplishment and the compliment I paid her.

"It'll be impressive if we can get over that hill tomorrow," she said. "My legs are like jelly."

"Mine too," I said rubbing my leg. My legs were sore, but food and rest would go a long way to help get us over the hill.

After we ate our pork we retired to the shelter to try and get a good night of sleep before tackling the monstrosity the next morning. Despite how tired I was, I could hardly sleep. Thoughts coursed through my mind one after another. I couldn't stop thinking about her. How she had saved my life, her glistening skin by the pool, and the kiss that could've been. It tormented my mind. There she was, mere inches from me and I could do nothing to quench my thoughts. I certainly didn't want to bring it up again, for fear of making her uncomfortable. The last thing that I wanted to do was make her uncomfortable. If I did, she could leave. I would be alone yet again. It wasn't worth it. I knew in my mind that I had just met her, and that she tormented me in the jungle to the point of insanity, but I didn't want to jeopardize losing her.

I rolled over toward her and watched her. I felt like a creep, but it calmed my mind. Her chest would heave up and down with each breath. She had a slight snore, cute and subtle. I thought about putting my arm around her, but knew that would be not only weird, but it would greatly violate her space. I didn't want to make an enemy out of her, or have her think I was some kind of weirdo that she

141

should distance herself from. I was beginning to think I was a weirdo, staring at a sleeping girl I hardly knew and imagining myself holding her and kissing her.

I shook away the thoughts, closed my eyes, and before I knew it, I fell into a deep sleep.

"Coffee," Willow said rubbing her eyes awake the next morning. "I could really go for a nice cup of coffee."

"Ah, don't say that," I said rubbing the sleep from my eyes. "Although, I wouldn't turn down a delicious latte right now. Heck, I'd settle for gas station coffee."

"Same here," she said. "Hey, doesn't coffee grow in tropical places?"

"I don't know," I answered. "One can hope, right?"

"Yeah," she said somewhat disappointed I didn't know the answer.

We left the camp and headed up the hill. It was a grueling experience that pained us every single step. Because of the storm the day before, the hill was slick with mud and wet debris. This made for troublesome traveling. Each step we would either sink into the mud a little or slide back down a couple feet. It was very frustrating. Somehow, though, we made it to the top.

The view was stunning. You could see the jungle stretch out and fade into a sandy beach. The beach then faded into crisp blue ocean. We could see a hundred miles of ocean water fading away toward the horizon. It felt like we were miles above sea level.

"You see that small clearing down there?" Willow asked while pointing at a spot between us and the beach.

"Yeah," I said.

"That's where we're going," she said. "The sheets of metal are in that field."

"Okay, let's do it," I said taking a breath and trying to mentally prepare myself for the trip.

We began our descent slowly, taking care to make sure each footing was properly supported. The ground was still very slick and muddy. The side of the hill was rather bare compared to the opposing side. There was only a few rock outcrops and a small scatter of plants. Otherwise it was mainly just sodden, muddy earth.

I was ahead of Willow, making a good pace down the hill. We were over halfway down the beast when I heard a sudden shriek. I turned around to see Willow sliding down the hill at an alarming speed. She had lost her footing, slipped, and gravity took over.

"Willow," I yelled. She came close to me and I tried to reach out and grab her hand but I was just a foot or so too far from her. Her body slid and rolled and toppled and twisted as it flew down the muddy hill. Panicking, I began to speed up my descent, although still trying to take care to mind my footings. I kept an eye on her as she rolled but when she got to the bottom she seemed to be swallowed up in the thick brush at the bottom.

When I reached the bottom I shouted her name, but there was no answer. My heart was racing, sweat poured from my face, and fear engulfed my mind. I couldn't see her in the dense brush and I feared the worst. I didn't want to find her dead. I didn't want her to become a short moment in my life. I couldn't stand the thought of being alone again, left to rot on this island all alone.

"Willow," I screamed. "Where are you?" It was then that I saw the faint shape of her body under a gathering of vines. I had never ran so fast. When I got to her, she was lifeless. There was a small stream of blood trickling from a cut on her head. It looked superficial, however, but I wasn't sure what damage had been done internally. "Willow? Are you okay?" She didn't respond. I tried to gather my thoughts and think of what to do. I checked for a pulse. I could feel a slight undulation. I was relieved. But she wasn't moving, or awake, or anything. I stopped, focused, and looked at her chest. There was no movement. I couldn't see her breathing. She had a pulse but she wasn't breathing. I didn't know what to do to help her.

"Please wake up, Willow," I pleaded. "I can't do this without you." Adrenaline was coursing through my veins. Thoughts of what to do clouded my mind. I began to speak aloud, asking her for guidance, as if she would respond. "Should I move you? No, you could have broken bones. Or worse, a broken neck. If I moved you, I could make it worse. Should I do CPR? Yes, that's it. You have a pulse but you aren't breathing. I need to do CPR. I used to lifeguard at a pool, so I know what to do." But the truth was, I lifeguarded so long ago, I was unsure if I still remembered how to perform the lifesaving task. But at that point, doing something was better than doing nothing at all. "But wait," I said to her. "You have a heartbeat, so chest compressions won't do any good. I've got to do mouth to mouth."

I kneeled over her motionless body. I brought my mouth to her mouth, closing her nose with my right hand. With my left hand I very gently lifted her head up, to open the airway. I took a deep breath and exhaled it into her mouth. I could see her chest lifting in my peripheral vision. I took another deep breath and gave it to her. Her chest again expanded, but then nothing. She still wouldn't breathe.

"Come on, Willow," I said. I stopped to make sure her heart was still beating. Thankfully, it was. I gave her another breath. Her chest again lifted, but she didn't start breathing. "Come on, you can do it. I need you." I gave her another breath and then her body twitched and convulsed. Then I heard the most amazing sound. She began coughing. She sat up, eyes still closed, and she was coughing. "Yes, that's it, breathe," I said happily.

In between coughs she managed to speak, "What happened?" A fit of coughs quickly followed.

"Oh, Willow," I exclaimed. "You did it."

"Did what?" Willow said through a veil of coughs. Her eyes finally opened and looked into mine. Her coughs subsided. "What did I do?"

"You came back," I said. "You weren't breathing."

"I was dead?" She said frightened.

"No, you had a heartbeat, but you weren't breathing," I answered.

"What happened?" She asked.

"You fell down the hill and must've hit your head or something. You weren't breathing," I said. I tore a piece of my shirt and wiped a small stream of blood that was emanating from her forehead.

"Wow, seriously?" She said placing her hand to the cut on her head.

"Yeah, you about scared me half to death," I said. She tried to stand up and began to lose her balance. "No, you need to rest for a little bit."

"No, I'm fine really," she said. "Just a little dizzy, that's all. I'll be okay."

"You could have a concussion," I surmised. "We'll just stay here for a while so you rest a little. And then, if you feel better in like a half hour or so, we'll head out. We still have plenty of daylight."

"Okay," she said. "Do you have any water on you?"

"Yeah, I think there's a little here," I said, pulling the water bottle from my pocket. She drank deeply, as if it was her first drink in days. Before I knew it, once solitary drip was left and she quickly shook the bottle so that it too would fall into her mouth. "Wow. You were thirsty, weren't you?"

"Yeah, sorry," she said with a giggle. "I don't know what came over me."

After an hour or so, the sun was hanging low in the sky, and it was time for us to move on. Willow's hand gripped mine and I yanked her up from the jungle floor. Her step was still a little unbalanced, but she managed to keep up a steady pace.

The trees at the bottom of the hill began to thin out and just randomly dotted the landscape, revealing a large biome. Tall grasses, brightly colored flowers of unusual shape and color, and the occasional small gathering of what appeared to be some sort of bushes laid out before Willow and I.

"There," Willow said, pointing to an oddly shaped bush. "There it is."

"There what is?" I asked, confused. "That's just a bush." It was thick, dense, and about ten feet across by roughly ten feet high. A thicket of grass was the only thing between us and the bush, which was about 30 yards away.

"No, you idiot," she said playfully. "Behind the bush, on the other side. That's where the metal is. I'm sure of it." Willow began to jog toward the bush and I followed, both of us were beaming with excitement. Her gait was accented by a slight limp, but it didn't seem to bother her.

The idea that just behind a bush was actual metal sheets, was quite thrilling. After many storms and only using palm fronds or big trees as a means to shelter from the rain, the prospect of having something sturdy and sheltering really lifted our spirits. It was quite surprising to see Willow running at such a swift speed after her near-death fall. But I figured if she thought she was okay enough to jog then it must not have been all that bad.

The bushes obscured the view of three large pieces of what seemed to be corrugated metal roofing. There were numerous holes in the sheets, although none were much bigger than a silver dollar. A brownish patina covered the metal like a bad rash. I grabbed one of the pieces to gauge its weight, giving it a slight lift.

"They're a little rickety," I said hesitantly. While the pieces were decent-sized, their overall condition wasn't the best. Besides the small holes, which would allow for water to drip in, the edges of the metal were so badly aged that they crumbled at the slightest touch.

"It's better than nothing," Willow said with a hint of defensiveness.

"Yeah, that's true," I agreed. "They'll do just fine for what we need them for. Maybe we can patch the holes somehow."

"We could just lay palm fronds over the holes," Willow replied.

"That would work, but I want this to be as close to stormproof as we can get," I said confidently.

"How are we going to make them stormproof?" Willow asked.

"Hmm...," I said. I was silent for a moment, thinking for an answer. I hadn't really thought my comment through and didn't want to sound like an idiot. "I know, we can get some sap from a tree and heat it up. Then coat a piece of fabric with the sap and patch the holes." I felt proud with my answer, especially considering it was on the spot.

"Wow," Willow exclaimed. "That's actually a really good idea."

"I'm full of good ideas," I said with an air of egotism.

"You're full of something," Willow said, followed by a cute chuckle.

"You better watch it," I said jokingly. We both shared a laugh.

"Come one, ya goof," Willow said nudging me. "We have to get this stuff back to our camp."

"Yeah," I said. "That's not going to be fun.

CHAPTER SEVENTEEN

Years ago, I had given up hope of being rescued from Nightmare Island. It was even to the point where I was going to end my own life. But years later, there I was watching the sunset with Willow, the woman who saved me, and I realized: love is a weird thing.

"Do you remember what it was like back in the real world?" Willow asked.

"What do you mean?" I said.

"You know, like where you lived before. The city, do you remember what it was like?" she reiterated.

"Compared to my life now, it was horrible," I said. "I was alone there. I mean, I had my family, but it was just me. Now I have you, the most beautiful view in the world, and a sort of life where everything we do we can be proud of."

"What do you mean?" she asked.

"Well, everything we have here: our cabin, the food we eat, the clothes we make, everything. It's stuff that wasn't just bought. We had to make it. We had to craft it with our hands," I said. "It wasn't just some mindless junk we got at a store, with no idea where it came from, how it was made, and who made it."

"That's very true," she said with a gleam in her eye. She laid her head on my shoulder and we both peered at the dancing ribbons of color before us. In that moment, there was a calm peacefulness.

"You know what I miss the most?" I asked her.

"What?" she said.

"Donuts," I answered.

"Oh, my gosh, Damon," she said laughing. "Of course that's what you miss."

"What? Donuts are delicious," I said with a chuckle. "You know how hard it would be to make a donut in this place? I'm not even sure it's possible."

"Yeah, it would not be easy," she said. "But, we could try."

"We would need some sort of flour, sugar, eggs, and oil," I said giving it an honest thought. "We could get the eggs by robbing a bird nest. Maybe we could substitute sugar by using some sweet fruit. But, the flour. That would be the hard part."

"Yeah, flour is something that would take some doing," she noted, running her delicate and tan hands through her long, sun-bleached hair.

"I wonder if we could dry that purple root that we use to make 'mashed potatoes'," I said. "If it was completely dry, we might be able to grind it into a powder to use like flour."

"That's genius!" Willow exclaimed. "Tomorrow, we'll get started, and, maybe very soon, we'll have some donuts."

"I can't wait!" I said, excitedly.

The sun was above the horizon, but quickly fading into deep amber colors that nestled in the azure of the sea. We gazed warmly at its brilliance, only feeling the movement of each other's breaths. The serene peace was quickly interrupted by Willow suddenly sitting up and staring off into the distance.

"Do you see that?" she asked.

"See what?" I said.

"There's something out there," she said lifting her head from my shoulder and peering intensely. "Right there, left of the sun." She pointed her fingers toward a small black shape in the distance.

"What the hell is that?" I asked.

"I don't know, but it looks like it's getting closer," Willow said. I stood up and walked a bit forward, trying to get a better view of the object. It appeared to be on the ocean and moving quick, but its shape was so unusual it was hard to tell what it was.

"Damon," Willow said with a hint of excitement. "It's a boat." I squinted my eyes and could finally make out its shape. It was a boat and it was heading our way.

"Oh my God," I whispered. "It is a boat."

"What do we do?" Willow said, her voice shrieking.

"You go light a torch and then go light the signal fire," I said. My hands were quivering and I could feel an intense nervousness and excitement begin to take hold of my emotions. "I'll get the flag and start waving it."

Willow ran towards our cabin to where our fire was gently flickering away and I ran toward the spot where we had planted our flag. It was a ten foot tall piece of bamboo that was stuck three feet into the ground and had a massive piece of fabric tied to its top. Scrawled across the fabric were the words: Nightmare Island. Below the name was a handprint from both Willow and I, with our name under each of our respective handprints. I gripped the bamboo pole with all my strength and yanked it from the ground. The flag and its pole were very heavy, but the adrenaline was coursing through my bloodstream and gave me the power to not only yank it from the ground, but also to run back to the beach and begin waving it toward the boat.

By this time, I could see out of my peripheral vision that Willow had successfully lit the signal fire and it was roaring tall and strong. The signal fire had sat in its same spot for months and months. Normally, we would change out the foliage for something fresh, so as to create a plume of smoke, but it had been so long that it burned bright, tall, and hot.

"Hey, we're over here!" I shouted at the top of my lungs. "Looks this way!"

Willow joined me at the water's edge and began screaming, too. "We're here. Right here!" she yelled. The boat seemed to be heading straight at us and was getting closer by the minute. Our voices were beginning to crack and wane from hollering, even though the likelihood that anyone on the boat could hear us was minimal at best.

Willow stopped yelling, but I continued the best I could. The boat was close, and had most certainly seen our efforts to get their attention. Suddenly, Willow gripped my forearm with an urgent passion.

"Damon, are they holding guns?" she said with a sort of horrifying calmness that made my excitement scatter into fear. I squinted my eyes, straining to focus on the boat. I could just barely make out several figures on the boat, each holding what appeared to be large guns. They were getting closer by the second.

"Oh, crap," I said. "Head for the jungle." I grabbed Willow's hand and began running toward the jungle as fast as I could. The sand, something I had gotten used to traversing, was a massive hindrance. It felt like I was stumbling in slow motion and making very little progress. A strange sound began ringing out, much like the snapping of a tree branches. It repeated over and over.

"They're shooting at us," Willow howled. We were almost to the edge of the beach, where the jungle begins, when I felt it. A sting in my back right calf. It was like hot pliers digging into me. My leg buckled and I fell and rolled into the sand, right on the cusp of the jungle. Because I was holding Willow's hand so tightly, she fell with me. A scream released from my mouth and I grasped at my leg. A dark scarlet liquid poured from the wound. More than I have ever seen in any situation in my life.

"Oh my God, I've been hit," I screamed. The sand was like a sponge, soaking up the blood with ease and staining its grainy surface crimson.

"Come on, we have to go," Willow said standing and pulling me to my feet. She put my arm around her shoulder and helped me get into the jungle. We ran and ran, not even paying any attention to where we were going. I was basically being directed by her, as I was in so much pain I couldn't think straight. The jungle seemed to be an amalgamation of plants, shades, and colors that zoomed by as we hurried ourselves to safety.

We reached a large fallen tree and Willow brought me around to the side of it that was away from where we ran.

"Here, sit down," she said breathing heavily. It was obvious that she was tired from running and supporting a majority of my body weight. Her breaths were short and shallow. Yet, even in all her tiredness, she reached down and began putting pressure on my wound, trying to keep the warm fluid from escaping my body. It still seeped out, staining the mossy jungle carpet.

"Go, Willow," I said. "Get out of here before they find us both."

"I am not leaving you," she said, her eyes pierced with fear.

"Yes, you need to get the hell out of here, now!" I yelled. "I don't want them to find you, too." My eyes felt heavy. Not like I was sleepy, but like I had consumed too much alcohol. I could feel it prying at me. Death. It's cold and firm grip clutching me more and more as the time passed.

"Willow, do this for me. Just go. Be safe. I love you." I felt her brush my face with a gentle, smooth motion.

"I'll come back for you, Damon," I heard her say. "I love you."

The grip of death's hands squeezed harder and my vision faded.

Then, it was dark. Everything went numb and inky black.

CHAPTER EIGHTEEN

One of the things I have always loved about camping was the simple pleasure of a campfire. But even more, the smell of a campfire. There's something calming, almost euphoric, about the woodsy pine smoke wafting up and filling the air. The smell gets stuck in your clothes, and while in normal life the smell is obtrusive, while you're camping it's almost a rite of passage.

I could the smell the fire, tingling at my nostrils and filling my mind with nostalgia. My eyes were closed, but I was beginning to wake from an unusual sleep. Then, before my eyes could open, I realized what had happened to me. I was shot. I was dead. Wasn't I? Why was I smelling campfire? I thought for a moment that maybe I did die, and the smell was the afterlife. But what kind of afterlife smells of fire. I didn't dare to continue thinking about it.

My eyelids lifted slowly, letting in a flood of white light. It was superbly bright, blotting out any chance of me being able to see what's around me. My mouth felt strange, like it was swollen, or like something was in it, blocking my ability to close it completely. I tried to speak, but couldn't say anything. I was sure there was something in my mouth.

"Hey, Captain, he's coming to," a strange voice said, startling me. My eyes had not yet fully adjusted, but I could see the shape of a person hovering over me. I tried to use my hands to stand myself up, but they were completely numb. I struggled as my memory came back to me. I remembered the boat, the people, their guns, the searing hot pain in my leg. I tried to scream, but it was muffled. It was obvious that I had a gag in my mouth. The shape of another person came within my view, which was getting better every moment. From the outline of him, he was much taller than the other person.

"Hey, there little fella," the man said. "How ya feeling?" His voice was raspy, like a seasoned smoker, and there was a tinge of an accent, although I couldn't figure it out. "You've had quite the time, haven't you?" I struggled, trying to say something, but the gag prevented that, and the only thing that would come out was a muffled mumble.

"Seems like we have a fighter in this one, wouldn't you say, Captain?" The other man spoke with a high-pitched drawl and was clearly lower on whatever ranking system the men had.

"Yes, we do," the deep voice boomed. "Well, enough with the pleasantries. I'm Captain Edwards. We're purveyors of unwanted things. Or, I guess, what most people would call pirates." The look on my face must have given away how idiotic and almost insane that sounded. "Now see here. There's no need for dirty looks. We're no swashbucklers if that's what you're thinking. We're bonafide

156

professionals. We enjoy traveling around and taking things that people don't need." My vision was now fully clear, and I could see that Captain Edwards was a tall, dirty man with scraggly beard and black eyes that sunk back into his skull. "Now, we came to this island for a little R&R, but then we saw your nice little smoke signals and thought we'd stop in to say hello. It wasn't very nice of you to run away like you did."

Willow, I thought. Where was Willow? I turned my head from the Captain and saw a horrendous sight. The cabin that Willow and I had built with our bare hands was burning, and Willow was lying unconscious right next to it. I fought to release myself, but I couldn't.

"Whoa there, little guy," the Captain said. "There's no need for you to get all up in arms. You see, we like things that make us money. It really pisses us off when we go out of our way to secure an investment and come to find out that investment is worthless. It makes us feel like we're being screwed over. As professionals, we don't enjoy being screwed over. That's the situation we find ourselves in now, unfortunately. While you were sleeping so peacefully, I had our ship doctor patch ya up, and we took a look around at all the marvels you've created since you've been here. It's been quite a while, hasn't it? Well, in that time you've amassed a big pile of crap. There's nothing of value for us, and that really pisses me off. So, we've made this simple for you. Normally, keep in mind, we'd just kill you if you didn't have anything for us. But, since we're nice guys and since killing you would end your misery on this godforsaken rock, we've decided to just burn everything you do have and leave you here to die, a slow painful death." I screamed as loud as I could, but nothing worthwhile would pass the gag. I looked back at Willow, she looked so peaceful, sleeping up against our aflame cabin. But soon, the fire would spread to where she was and she would be burned alive. I struggled again, but I began to accept defeat. A tear rolled down my cheek, as salty as the ocean waves. "Well, isn't that sweet," the Captain said sarcastically. "You seem genuinely worried about the current state of things. Now, I'm not a monster. I won't leave you here bound and gagged with everything you love burning all around you. I will throw you a little bone. You see that log over there?" I looked to where the Captain was pointing and there was a log of driftwood with a knife sticking out of it. "Yeah, that one. That knife is for you. We're going to head on out of here. When we're gone, feel free to wiggle your worthless little self over to that knife. It's a good knife. Call it payment for shooting you in the leg. Sorry about that, by the way. You ran and we reacted. My chums are nothing if not good shots."

"Captain, we got to go. Radio says a storm's coming," another voice said from out of my view.

"Well, son, you're on your own, again," the Captain said to me, with a pat on my leg. "I want to thank you for the nice talk. It was refreshing having someone just listen to me and not babble on about this or that. I wish you the best of luck here. And hey, maybe one day we can find each other and have a nice drink together and laugh about this day." Hate poured from my eyes and shot at the Captain with an almost feverish passion. The Captain turned and began walking away. In the shallow waves, a small raft with a man in it was waiting. The Captain and the other man got in. With one more horrid look, the Captain stared at me straight in the eyes and then winked. It was like salt in an already searing wound. The raft sputtered away and headed toward a bigger boat in the distance.

The smoke was billowing up into the sky and the flames on the cabin were burning a bright orange. Willow was still passed out, but the fire was so close to her that it wouldn't be long before she was consumed along with the cabin. I rolled from where I was and began teetering toward the knife that was stabbed in the log. The dry, loose sand made my task quite difficult, but I made my way. I had to sit myself up against the log so that I could reach the knife. As carefully and quickly as I could, I used the stuck blade of the knife to saw away at the ropes around my wrists. After what seemed like a lifetime, the rope gave and my hands were free. I pulled the gag from my mouth and then yanked the knife from the driftwood and sawed at the rope around my ankles. After I was completely free I hobbled toward the burning cabin and Willow. The cabin was completely engulfed. The fire was burning right next to Willow and I could see that her hair was beginning to smolder and singe. I grabbed her lifeless arms and dragged her safely away from the burning cabin we called home.

"Willow," I yelled. There was no change in her consciousness. "Willow, wake up." I felt her neck for a heartbeat. I could faintly feel the thumping of her heart. She was alive. A wave of relief poured through my body. I shook her again and saw that her eyes were opening. "Willow, it's me."

"Damon?" She mumbled.

"Yes, it's me my love," I replied with a smile. "Thank God you're okay." She started to sit up.

"What's going on?" She said rubbing the fog from her eyes.

"We were attacked," I said stroking her head. "By pirates." She let out a sharp laugh and her eyebrows furled.

"What are you talking about?" She said. "Pirates?"

"Yeah, pirates," I said. "They said they came here to relax and when they saw us they took the opportunity to try and steal from us. But, what happened to you? The last I remember before passing out was you running away to hide."

"I did hide, but they found me," she said. "I was in these bushes laying down, hoping they wouldn't see me. I could hear them searching for me, but I didn't make a sound. But as I was laying there, I heard the bush I was in rustle. I looked up and saw a man and then, I don't know. I must've passed out or something." It was then that Willow looked around and noticed our cabin on fire. "Oh my God, what happened to our home?"

"They set it on fire," I said. "I guess it was our punishment for not having anything valuable. They put you next to it, and if I hadn't got to you sooner you would've..." I trailed off, not daring to finish the sentence.

"How come they didn't just kill us?" She asked.

"The Captain said it was because he figured it was a worse fate to be stuck here without anything," I said.

"The Captain?" Willow said confused.

"Yeah, Captain Edwards, to be exact," I replied. Willow chuckled and rolled her eyes.

"You weren't kidding, were you?" She said. "We really were attacked by pirates."

"Yeah we were," I said. "Of all the things, pirates!"

"Wait, you were shot," she said suddenly and with grave concern. She looked at my leg, which was nicely patched up. She felt the bandages, as if she could determine its condition with her soft touch. "Did they fix you up?"

"Yeah, Captain Edwards said their doctor fixed me and then had the audacity to apologize for shooting me," I said.

"Hopefully they did a good job. It could easily get infected here," she mentioned with a concerned tone.

"Yeah, I know. I'll take good care of it," I said. "But my leg is not our biggest concern right now. What are we going to do about our home?"

"I have no idea," she simply said. A thwack of thunder rang out and the sky became dark with an ominous blanket of clouds. The sound startled us both.

"I did hear one of them say a storm was coming," I said. "I guess they were right. We need to find shelter."

We headed inland for the trees. My leg rung out in deep pain with every step, making getting anywhere especially difficult. It was like sharp bolts of lightning stabbing away at me. Each movement was another excruciating shock of anguish and suffering that only seemed to get worse with each passing moment. It was something that I just had to deal with it to make sure that Willow and I got somewhere we could shelter from the dark storm that nipped at our heals.

"Where are we going to go?" Willow asked.

"Let's go to the cave," I responded gritting my teeth torment. "We can stay there until we figure things out and this storm passes."

"Are you alright?" Willow asked.

"I'll be fine," I said trying to put on a brave face. "Let's just get there and worry about everything else then."

"Okay," Willow said, but with a concerned looked.

The journey was arduous. The storm caught up with us and released a torrential downpour that hit the ground with such a velocity that droplets of water seemed to bounce upwards at us. We were soaked from head to toe. It was miserable.

The cabin we built was practically waterproof and we never had to worry about the elements, but it was gone. Reduced to rubble and ashes. The home we shared so many beautiful moments in was no more. The thought of it brought a tear to my eye, which was quickly swept away by the pouring rain.

The cave had changed since the last time that we visited it, years ago. We had only been to it a couple times, before our cabin was built and only when the island was engulfed in storms so bad that sheltering in it was the wisest choice.

"Our handprints are gone," I said pointing to the smooth rock wall. "Just like everything else we have worked so hard to get."

"Everything we had we can get back," she said helping me sit. "This isn't an end to something, it's a different beginning. We'll come back from this, stronger than before."

"Do you still love me?" I asked.

"Of course I do," she said. "Why would ask something like that?"

"I couldn't protect us," I said weakly. "We could've died because I wasn't strong enough to save us."

"There was nothing you could've done to make that go any differently," she said sternly. "You did what you could, and I love you even more for it."

"I didn't do anything," I said dropping my eyes to the cave floor.

"Damon," she said lifting my head up and making me look into her gentle eyes. "You told me to go. You sacrificed yourself. If anything, I left you all alone."

"I should've done more," I said.

"You did enough," she said proudly with a sharp smile. "We're here now. It's over. They're gone, and, with any luck, their ship is getting pounded by this storm. But we're still here. We will rebuild our cabin. We'll get more supplies."

"I guess you're right," I said. "We can rebuild. We can even make things even better than they were."

162

"Yeah, maybe you can build me that second story like I've been asking for," she said with a chuckle and a playful bump to my arm with her elbow.

"It's a deal," I said smiling. "I love you, Willow. I don't what I'd do without you." I took hold of her hand in mine, my thumb slowly caressing the top of her hand. She leaned in and gave me a soft kiss on the cheek. It was everything. It was medicine. We were one soul and nothing could change that. Not Nightmare Island, not pirates, nothing.

The storm raged on outside our cave sanctuary for what seemed like hours, but in all reality, it was peaceful. We sat silently, holding each other and listening the downpour. The light was fading minute by minute, but neither of us made any effort to make a fire. We had accepted our temporary fate of damp clothes, broken homes, and bullet holes. In fact, we embraced it. The test we were put through only made us stronger as a unit. If Willow wasn't with me, I would've given up. I would have no reason to continue. The island would win the battle against me. But, with Willow, it was like she was a fortress wall that kept all the bad things and bad thoughts away. Now, the only things that were running through my head were how much I love her and what I can do to keep her safe. What's the point of having a fortress wall if you're not protecting it from being chipped away?

CHAPTER NINETEEN

I t was the fourth straight week of Willow's sickness. To say I was worried would've been an extreme understatement. Living on an island with an unsteady food supply was one thing, but to be constantly throwing up was another. I figured if something didn't change soon, there was a real possibility that she could starve to death.

I did my best to try and keep her comfortable. While I was busy putting the finishing touches on our new house, she rested in our makeshift hut. I would take frequent breaks and make sure she was drinking water and trying to eat something. She was weak, tired, ill, and I could do nothing to help her. She needed a doctor, which, because of our situation, had to be me. I did my best, but I thought the worst. Somehow she got sick from something. What? I had no idea. But I knew that Nightmare Island was trying to take her from me. It's what it did best. It gives and it takes away.

"Willow," I said kneeling beside our palm frond bed. "Wake up. You need to drink some water." Her eyes opened slowly and struggled to focus on me. The sound of the dried fronds crunching as she turned from her side seemed to echo throughout the hut, overtaking the sounds of the jungle around us.

"What time is it?" She asked. Her hands were weak, but still found the strength to rub the fog from her eyes.

"I'd say about noon," I replied stroking her hair, which was knotted and tangled from heavy sleeping. "Here, sit up and have a drink." She pulled herself up, her back against the hut. Each gulp of water she drank filled me with hope. Today could be the day her sickness ends, I thought. But before my hope could be fully realized, she handed me the water and spewed it all back up all over the hut floor. I quickly held her hair back and stroked her back, as if either of those things would do more than comfort.

"I'm sorry, Damon," she said. Her eyes were watering from the expulsion and they dove deeply into my heart.

"You have nothing to be sorry about," I said. "I just wish I could take this pain away and make you better again." A sort of sickly smile formed from her mouth, but quickly faded.

"So do I," she said. "I just want this to end. I don't know what's wrong with me. One day I'm fine and then the next I can hardly move. I'm so tired."

"We'll get through this, I promise," I said. "You should get some more rest. I'll go back to work on the house. I'll be back to check on you in an hour or so, okay?" I said.

"Okay," she said. "I can't wait to see it. It's been so long that I can't even remember what it looks like."

166

"When you're feeling better I'll give you a tour," I said. "Until then, sleep well and dream well." She laid her head down and seemed to drift off to sleep instantly.

Her sickness broke my heart. It hurt my soul. She was what gave me strength. She was my superpower. Seeing her in such a state was heartbreaking. Unfortunately, however, there was nothing I could do to help her, aside from giving her water, food, rest, and comfort. I was, in a sense, just as helpless as she was lying on our bed.

Building our house occupied a lot of my energy and thoughts. It was grand. A two-story monstrosity made out of the best jungle wood I could find. The bottom floor was a large square room that contained what would essentially store goods, including a deep hole lined with palm fronds that served as a makeshift refrigerator. The hole was roughly six feet deep and had a ladder that led down into it. Surprising, in the jungle heat and humidity, it was rather cold, and I felt that it would extend the life of our food supplies a considerable amount of time. Spoilage in the jungle was a serious issue. The lifespan of any food was short in the humidity. It was, after all, the perfect breeding ground for bacteria that wreak havoc on the body. The bottom floor would also serve as a place to weather storms. I used the biggest trees I could maneuver as a foundation. I came up with a sort of pulley system to get the trees to the location I needed them to, and then used whatever thick branches I could find to leverage them into place. It was as sturdy as I could make it without adding a proper cement foundation.

The top story was built for Willow. It was her dream bedroom. Well, her dream bedroom considering the circumstances. Living on an island with almost no actual building supplies, furniture, or decorations make it hard to build a real dream anything, let alone a bedroom.

The room's floor was made from a type of strong bamboo. Because the bamboo was cylindrical, it left grooves that I filled with mud. While the mud was still wet I added the fibers from the inside of a coconut husk to make it look and feel like a sort of coarse carpet. It did the trick and made for a quite comfortable flooring. It reminded me of my previous life. The life I had before Nightmare Island. That life, however, wasn't real. Everything I had was fake, built and made for me by someone I'd never meet. The house, the carpet, the bed, the blankets, everything. Every single thing I just bought or rented. Nothing was mine. Nothing was made from my own two hands. But Nightmare Island, it was different. Everything was made by me. There was a sense of pride. It was nice looking at something that you made from start to finish and thinking, I did that. All of it.

The top floor, Willow's dream bedroom, had it all. I built the bed from bamboo, laying out palm fronds over a supporting frame. It wasn't a big box store mattress, but it was comfortable. When the pirates burned down our original cabin, the metal roofing that we travelled so far to get was ruined. Although, a big piece of it remained intact. Not good enough for roofing, but good enough for a mirror. With the roofing laid out on the ground I covered it in sand and used a piece of my shirt to grind the sand into the surface of the metal. This took away all of the rust and soot from the fire and left the surface a dull grey color. From there I took some fine dirt, free of any clumps, and repeated the process. I continued for three days, doing this with various things that were finer and finer until I could see a sort of reflection in the metal. It wasn't a mirror, by any stretch, but it would work. I hung it in her dream room on the wall adjacent to the foot of the bed.

Outside of the house I dug another hole, this one even deeper than the fridge hole. It was maybe 12 feet deep. I used a ladder to get in and out of the hole, which also served as a way to remove the loose dirt. After the hole was dug, I built a small shed-like structure over it to serve as a bathroom. There was even a platform that could be sat upon with a hole that would allow waste to drop into the deep hole. A small mound of dirt and a homemade shovel could be used to cover the waste that fell below. Everything about this house was just perfect. I was proud. I knew Willow would be proud when she got better and could see it. It would be our home.

But would she ever get better, I worried. I thought of all the things that could possibly be making her sick. The one that stood out was the most daunting of all the things I would consider. Malaria. It was real, and it was deadly. My heart scattered to ashes thinking about it. No, I thought, it's just food poisoning. But I knew in deep in my mind it wasn't food poisoning. That only lasts for a few days, maybe a week. This, whatever this was, was going on over a month and it wasn't getting better. She seemed to be sick all the time. She was always tired and weak. Most of the time she threw up her food and water, although other times she was able to get it down. Just enough. Just enough so that she wouldn't starve, but it was close, I knew that much. Malaria. It was a horrible word. It was a horrible thing. How could something so deadly come from something so small? The culprits were everywhere. They were always everywhere. I had gotten used to the mosquitos swarming around me, taking small samples of my blood as I worked, slept, and survived. They were always there. Even before Willow, they were there. I was never truly alone. They were with me. Swarming about, feasting off my dwindled supply. In some way, I was the mosquito for Nightmare Island. I would suckle off anything I could get my hands on. But, unlike myself, I wasn't able to poison and kill the island with a slow and painful death. Just one mosquito with malaria and it's over. Sometimes, from things I read years ago, even treatment wouldn't help, and we might as well have been on another planet. There was no treatment for Willow. There was just me, and I was of little help. I tried not to let too much of my despair show to Willow. I needed to be strong for her. I was all she had. If it was malaria, I would soon be alone again. Another hole would need to be dug, this one much more cruel and somber. It would be a grave. A grave for the only person in my entire world that meant anything to me. Willow. My sweet Willow.

A tear swelled in my eye. She's going to die, I thought. The thought surprised me. I didn't choose to think it. It just happened, against my will. The thought originated in my head as a whisper, but soon grew to a scream. It was so booming I thought for sure it would escape into the world around me, but it didn't. It stayed bricked-in within my mind. I wouldn't let it escape. I couldn't. If I said it aloud it might make it true. It might become real with just a single, soft utterance. No, I thought forcefully, nothing is going to take her away from me.

"Nothing," I said to myself. "Nothing will take her from me." Saying those words out loud felt good. It felt like it made them real, and not the grim ones.

I continued working. Just about everything with the house was done, with exception to the roof. The utmost care had to go into the roof. I made it out of a base layer of bamboo split in half and laid upside down, so as to make a sort of gutter that would funnel rain away from the inside of the house. But, as added security, I laid palm fronds on top of the bamboo. Then, on top of the fronds, I put down a thick layer of mud, followed by more fronds, mud, and finally more fronds that were tied down to each other and then to more bamboo

170

that held everything down. The roof was as waterproof as it could be. Some water would likely get through, but it wouldn't be all that much.

I was adding some more large pieces of bamboo that would serve to hold everything down in heavy winds when I was startled by a sudden weak-sounding voice.

"Damon," Willow said. "It's amazing."

"Willow," I said. "What are you doing?" I climbed down my rickety ladder to speak with her face to face. Her skin was pale and sickly, but she seemed to smile with a beautiful glow.

"You've done such a good job. It's beautiful," she said, spreading her hands at the house.

"Willow, what are you doing?" I asked. "You need to be resting." I embraced her gently and looked into her eyes. Her beautiful eyes. Nothing would take those eyes from me. Nothing.

"I think I know what's wrong with me," she said.

"What do you mean?" I asked perplexed. "What's wrong with you?"

"I think I'm pregnant," she said.

CHAPTER
TWENTY

As I sat on the edge of our bed, I noticed that she had such beauty when she slept. The subtle rise and fall of her chest with each life-giving breath. There was a wispy reverberation that escaped her mouth, like the boiling of a jolting teapot without the whistle. Not quite a snore, but not just breaths. It was a breath of dreams, comfort, a breath of peace.

Willow had a certain grace about her that was only accentuated by the glow of her pregnancy. It had only been a few months since she told me she was pregnant. Our child was growing inside her, quickly, as evidenced by the cute belly-bump that grew further away from her body.

I was scared. Not necessarily scared to be a father. I mean, that was certainly there, but it was more than that. I was scared for the baby's quality of life. Nightmare Island wasn't the best place in the world to live as an adult, let alone as a baby. It would be hard. Food, clean water, even diapers were something that we were going to have to be figured out and would be needed in steady supply. A baby doesn't understand why there's no food. If the fish aren't biting, or fruits aren't ripe, or we can't find any wild animals, the baby won't understand that. They won't just be okay with waiting and being hungry. And they shouldn't have to either.

A lot of work needed to be done. I was contemplating trying to figure out how to go about catching a couple wild pigs and breeding them for food. I wasn't even sure it was possible. There are wild, after all. It's possible that domestication isn't even possible. There were a lot variables. A lot of variables for a lot of things. It wasn't always black and white, and it wasn't always a shade of grey. Some days there was food and clean water. Some days there was one or the other. Some days there was nothing at all. Nothing about Nightmare Island was steady, or consistent, or even sane. It was always hectic, all the time. It was like walking into a wave. Certain times were calm and everything seemed slow and at peace, but other times were tumultuous, getting hit left and right with frothy uncertainty. No baby should have to endure a life of such unreliability. It was my job to make sure that our child was safe and well taken care of. It would be a job that I would refuse to fail at.

"Don't look so concerned," Willow said, stretching her arms out in front of herself. "We'll be fine. You, me, and especially our baby. We will be fine." She gently rubbed my knee.

"What? How did you? It's like you read my mind," I said slightly taken aback. It was almost like she could tell exactly what I was thinking just by the look on my face.

"You don't have a very good poker face, you know," she said with a chuckle. "But really, we'll be fine. Our hearts beat as one. We both share the same kind, loving, and deeply caring soul. Our baby will be fine. We'll weather whatever storm comes our way, together."

"You're right," I said. "I'm just worried about the things we can't handle. Like, what if we need a doctor because the baby's sick or something?"

"That's a scary thought," she said somberly. "But, that's a bridge we don't have to cross until we're right up on it. We'll do our best. People have been having babies by themselves long before doctors."

"That's true," I said. Of course, she was right. Even if I wanted to vent about how scared I was and talk about all the what-ifs, there was no point in putting that stress on her. She felt it, too. That was apparent. Adding more wouldn't help the situation at all. I knew that the best thing that I could do was to prepare for the worst and hope for the best.

"So, what are we going to do today?" Willow asked, changing the subject.

"I figured we could go down to the ocean and try and catch some fish," I said. "I want to try and dry it into fish jerky. Or, maybe I could try smoking it. If you're up to fishing we could probably catch quite a few. Some to eat for the next couple of days and some to dry and smoke."

"That sounds good," Willow said. "Let's head out."

Our cabin wasn't too far from the beach, but far enough in the jungle that no one would be able to notice that we were there. After the pirates, we were a little paranoid about being seen again. It wasn't that we didn't want to be seen, we just wanted to make sure that we were cautious about who saw us. I figured that if those same pirates decided to come back, they would probably be a little more violent than they were last time. We just didn't want to risk more than we needed to, especially with a baby on the way.

175

We peered out from the edge of the jungle. I stole a glance at Willow. She gently pressed her face into the bushes until she just could barely see out from them. The bushes hardly even moved. It made me think about all the times I would see eyes staring at me from the jungle. That's how she would do it, I thought. There was something ninja-like about her furtiveness as she scanned the beach and sea. She must've felt me staring at her and turned and caught me, validating her suspicions.

"What?" She asked. "You look like you've seen a ghost."

"Sorry," I said shaking away my gaze. "I was just watching you stare out and I thought of all the times you would do that to me while I was alone."

"I'm pretty good at that, aren't I?" She said playfully. "You had no idea you weren't alone."

"Oh, I knew," I said. "You weren't that good. I mean, you were decent, but I knew you were there." We both smirked at each other. "I think it's safe. Shall we?" I said, parting a snag of branches for her to walk through.

"Well, thank you my king," she said with a graceful curtsey. I gave a slight and playful bow as she walked onto the beach.

The fishing was really good. We had caught about a dozen small fish of varying sizes and types. We had no idea what kind of fish they were. We just knew they were edible, or so we hoped. Some were brightly colored. Some were dull and shaped strangely. One of them was even flat, with its eyes on the top of the body and its mouth on the bottom of the body. It was a strange looking fish, but it would make for some easy jerky. After all, it was already flat and skinny.

We were treading water, about hip-high when I noticed a slight hum begin to fill the air, like a swarm of bees in the distance, growing closer every moment. I stopped what I was doing and listened

176

intently, looking around to see if I could spot where the sound was coming from.

"Willow, do you hear that?" I asked.

"Hear what?" She replied.

"That buzzing, or humming sound," I said.

"I don't hear anything. Maybe it's in your head," she said.

"No, I don't think so," I said looking around with haste. "It seems to be getting louder. What the heck is that?"

"I think you're losing it," she said playfully while casting her fishing pole into the water.

Without warning, a large rubber raft with an almost comically large motor appeared from behind the cliff by where we were fishing. The boat contained two large men, one at the back controlling the motor, and the other toward the front of the boat, holding a fishing pole.

"Willow, run," I yelled. My voice carried and reverberated off the cliff and the two men saw us as we took off toward the beach. The wake of the water gave us no ease of movement. To the men on the boat, it probably appeared that we were running in slow motion. I looked back. The boat had already turned toward us and was catching up to us with extreme speed. I knew there was no way that we'd outrun them.

"Hey, it's okay," one of the men hollered. "We're not going to hurt you." Still we ran, as fast as we could. It would never be fast enough to outrun the sheer power and ferocity of the raft.

"Willow, you keep running for the jungle," I yelled. "I'll hold them off. Get somewhere safe."

"Damon, no, come with me," she yelled back.

"Willow, go, now," I yelled with stern passion. She kept running, but I stopped at the water's edge. The boat was coming to a stop right in front of me as I turned around to face our pursuers. The man piloting the boat shut the engine off and the man on the front hopped out of the raft, making a large splash in the water.

"Why'd you run?" The man said. "We weren't trying to scare you. We can help you."

"What do you want?" I said standing up straight and slightly puffing out my chest.

"Do you need help?" He asked.

"I guess that depends," I said. "How do I know you won't hurt us?"

"We won't hurt you. We can help you," he said. "How did you get here?"

"I was in a plane crash," I said. "There's one more person here with me and she's pregnant."

"Okay, well we can help you both," he said.

"Okay," I replied. "But I need to know that you're not going to hurt us."

"We are not bad people, I promise," he said with a genuine look on his face.

"Alright," I said. "I'm trusting you. I am prepared to defend us if something seems wrong, just so you know."

"I understand," he said.

"Okay," I said relaxing my stance a little. "What do we do?"

"Call it in," he said turning to the man by the motor. The man by the motor picked up a handheld radio and turned it out. It emitted a shower of static before he tuned it to the right channel.

"Hello," he said. "Do you read me? Is there anyone out there? This is the Captain of the Ezra Faye." There was silence for a moment before a voice came over the radio.

"Ezra Faye, this is the United States Navy," the voice said. "How can we help you?"

"We're on the western shore of Nomad's Island and we've to have found a person that has been stranded from a plane crash," he said into the radio. My heart was beating as fast and hard as a group of galloping horses.

"Copy that," the voice said. "Head east toward Rarotonga, we'll meet you along the way and pick them up. We're about two hours out."

"Copy that," the man said. "We'll see you soon. Thank you."

"No problem," the man on the radio said.

"You see," the man in front of me said. "That was the United States Navy. They have a small base in Rarotonga. We'll take you to them and you can go home. How long have you been here?"

"I don't know," I said, trying to piece it all together. "Years, I think."

"How many years?" He asked.

"I'm not quite sure," I said. "Three? No, four. No, that's not right. I guess, I don't know. I've lost track of time."

"Well, we'll take care of you," he said. "My name is Raul. Why don't you go get this other person and we can get you both home."

"Yeah," I said simply. I was in a sort of shock. After everything, I could finally go home. My mind reeled back at the thought. Everything Willow and I have been through was about to come to end. Everything would be fine. Our baby would get to live a normal life, with food, clean water, and everything else a baby needs.

I turned to begin walking back to get Willow when I saw her, standing at the jungle's edge. She looked frightened.

"Willow, come here," I said. She shook her head and stayed still, just staring at me from the fringe. "It's okay, they're going to take us home. We can finally go home."

She still didn't move. She just quickly shook her head. I started walking toward her and when I got close I noticed that she had tears streaming from her eyes.

"Hey, it's going to be okay," I said, wiping away her tears. "We get to go home. The man called the Navy and everything. They're going to meet us on the way to Rarotonga and take us home." I took hold of her hand and began walking back toward the men and their raft. I noticed them staring at me with furled eyebrows.

"Damon, are you sure it's safe," she said.

"If anything seems weird I will take care of it," I said. "I have my knife. Don't worry about anything, okay?"

"Hey, who is he talking to?" The man in the raft said. I saw Raul wave at him to stop talking. Willow and I reached Raul. She wouldn't look at him, her eyes fixed to the sandy shoreline.

"This is Willow," I said. Raul's face was a frightening pale white. "What's wrong? You look like you've seen a ghost."

"I hate to break this to you," Raul said. "But, there's no one there with you."

"What?" I said, baffled at such a notion. "What do you mean?"

"Listen," he said putting his hands on my shoulders. "You are alone. There's no one else here."

"Get off of me," I said shaking his hands from my shoulders and pulling out my knife. "Are you crazy? She's right here. Willow, say something." Willow slowly looked up from the sand and into my eyes.

"I'm sorry, Damon," she said. "But I can't go."

"What do you mean you can't go?" I said confused.

"I have to stay," she said. "I'm sorry. I'll always be with you. Well, we'll always be with you." She took my hand and placed it on her stomach.

"I don't understand," I said.

"Hey, we need to get out of here," the man in the boat said.

"It's time for us to go," Raul said.

"I'm not leaving without her," I said holding the knife towards the man.

"I'm sorry," Raul said with sincerity. "There is no her. There is only you."

"No, you're messing with me," I said.

"Raul, now," the man in the boat yelled. "With or without him."

"Please," he said. "Let's go.

"No, I am not going anywhere without her," I said pointing to Willow. Raul lunged out at me and grabbed me with his arms, making me drop the knife. He then pinned my arms down so I couldn't fight back, but I did. I squirmed as hard as I could, but I couldn't break his grip.

He hurled me over the side of the raft and the impact of hitting the wood-lined raft knocked the wind out of me. I desperately sat up to look at Willow. What I saw terrified me beyond belief.

Willow stood, ankles in the lapping waves, staring at me. She gently smiled and began to fade away, like a hologram. With a smile still on her face, she gave me a single wave before she faded away completely.

"Willow..." I screamed.

CHAPTER
TWENTY ONE

The plane hit the runway at an alarming speed. The flight from Rarotonga, courtesy of the United States Navy, was smooth and without cause for concern. However, my nerves were shot. I gripped the armrests of my chair with fiery intensity and every muscle in my body was tense and tight. It seemed like I was holding my breath the entire time, just waiting for something horrible to happen. After all, the last time I was on a plane it fell from the sky like it got too close to the sun and its wings were made of wax.

Tears suspended themselves in my eyes the entire flight. Not just from the shear fear of disaster, but also because my mind kept playing back every moment on Nightmare Island. The idea that Willow wasn't real made no sense. I could remember her smell, her touch, her gentle words, yet, she was never there. The idea of that made no sense. How was it possible that she was just in my mind? Nothing made any sense. The strangest feeling swept over my body. It was the feeling of loneliness. It was the same feeling that I had so long ago, before Willow, before I was happy, in love, and on the verge of becoming a father. All I wanted was to be back with her. To say I missed her would've been incorrect. I yearned for her. I needed her. But, she was never there. How can someone need someone that never existed?

"You said your name was Damon, right?" A short and stubby man asked me. I had barely spoken since leaving the island. I had no words. I was scared, embarrassed, and didn't know what to do. I had watched the people that had rescued me tell the Navy about my hallucinations and I saw their reactions. I've never seen someone's face go from concerned to confused so fast. Everyone that got near me gave me these penetrating glances, like they were trying to dissect my mind and figure out what happened. Suddenly, I wasn't just a stranded person on an island. Once they knew the truth about me and my time on Nightmare Island I became something else. I became insane. But I wasn't. I knew for a fact that I wasn't crazy, yet everyone looked at me like I should've been wearing a straitjacket and be put in a padded room, kept away from the sane people.

Before the flight home, a top-ranking Navy official tried to interview me. He asked me what happened when the plane went down, how I survived, and about Willow, or rather, the person I saw. To me she was my entire world, the love that kept my heart beating, but to everyone else she was the person I saw. A fictional delusion created in my mind to keep me entertained. The only thing I told the official was my name. Not only did I not want to talk to them because I was in a weird state of shock, but they wouldn't have wanted to hear what I had to say. They would lock me up for sure if I told them the truth. They could never understand my love for her and my unborn child. They could never see how deeply tormented I was without them. If I gave them the opportunity to see my truth, then I would certainly be taken away and put into some dark corner, away from the sights and minds of gawking people.

I sat silently in my seat, staring at the seat in front of me. The plane gently hummed as it made its way toward the airport. I could hear the stubby man talking to me, but I didn't care to respond to him.

"Okay," he said softly. "It's okay if you don't want talk. I just wanted to let you know that we just got word that your parents are here waiting to see you. There's also a lot of reporters, but we're going to keep them away from you so you can see your parents in peace."

For some reason his words were like knives. All this time I could only think of Willow and my time on Nightmare Island. But now, my parents were thrown into the mix. A stream of tears poured from my eyes, yet I remained like stone otherwise. Of course I had missed my parents, and I was sure that they missed me. I was sure that they thought I was gone, lost forever in the cool blue depths of the Pacific Ocean. But, here I was, minutes away from seeing them again. I was in no condition for reunions. My condition, however, was irrelevant. I would see them. I would go home with them. They would ask questions. Questions that I was not prepared to answer, or rather, didn't have answers to give them.

The plane came to a sudden stop and the engines winded down from its gentle hum to a silent vacancy. What seemed like a lifetime on Nightmare Island all at once came to an end. I was home. Or, at least, the place I had called home before the fateful journey of my grand adventure. What a grand adventure it was. Now it was over, despite the feelings I had that left me feeling incomplete. Willow should've been with me. We should be together. That was the plan if we were ever rescued. But instead, I was alone. Sure, my family was waiting for me just outside the plane, but I was different. The man they knew that left so long ago for his grand adventure was not the man that was about to return to them. They wouldn't understand, and I knew that I wouldn't ever be the same.

"Alright, are you ready?" The man said. He gestured me toward the door. A large, stressful breath escaped from deep inside my lungs and I stood from my seat.

Two men in military outfits opened the door of the plane and I stepped into the jet bridge, the walkway that connects a plane to the airport. The hall was stale, dim, and seemed to cascade endlessly toward my destiny. A destiny I yearned for, but not like this. This was not what I wanted, yet, there I was, fulfilling it. Each step was closer and closer to the unknown. As long as the jet bridge seemed to sprawl on, I journeyed its length rapidly. I turned the corner and entered the airport.

"Oh my God, Damon," my mom howled, her hair unevenly disheveled and tears rolling out from her eyes. They streamed and glistened like lapping waves against the sandy shores of her cheeks. My dad was no different. Both my parents ran at me from a distance, arms wide open, sad, confused, and ready to embrace the child they thought they lost. I was not ready.

They collided with me, and soon four arms were wrapped around me. My response was cold. I accepted their clutches, but returned nothing. I was empty. I could feel the love they offered me, but gave them none. It wasn't that I didn't want to, I did. I just couldn't. My scar was so deep that even their infinite pouring of love couldn't satiate the emptiness I suffered. There was no remedy for what I suffered.

They hugged me for what seemed like a hours. All the while, in the distance of the airport, reporters and their ilk hollered questions at me, along with a shower of flashing white lights from their prodding cameras. A line of what appeared to be security and police kept them from getting any closer. As my parents continued their embrace, I wondered if the world knew of Willow. I wondered if everyone knew that I had some sort of breakdown, delusion, or hallucination.

I stared off into the distance while my parents squeezed me tightly. In the background of the reporters, I saw her. It was certainly her. Willow. She was walking slowly away. I ripped myself from my parents and rushed over towards her. She was real, I knew it. I wasn't crazy. I piled into the reporters, pushing passed them with carelessness.

I got to her and grabbed her shoulders. She shrieked and as she turned to face me I saw that it was not her. It wasn't my sweet Willow. It was just some random person, whose eyes gazed at me curiously and judge my actions. I release her shoulders and turned to head back to my parents. The swarm of reporters that had by this time surrounded me, didn't faze me. I walked through their questions and camera flashes as if they too were as fake as Willow.

"Step aside, please," the stubby man said to the reporters as I reached the barrier. "Let him through."

"Willow," someone hollered. I quickly looked toward the person and saw a man and a woman embracing a young teen, probably 15 or 16 years old. It seemed that she had just got off her flight and was reuniting with her family. My heart shattered again. Fate played yet another joke on me. My Willow was not here, no matter how much I wanted her to be. She was gone. A memory only I would have.

The stubby man was lingering behind me, and after a while he spoke up. "If you'd like I can take you to a more private room," he said. My parents, who had watched me run off agreed with him. We were ushered off into a small, poorly lit room. It was cold and void of anything with exception to a single table and three metal chairs. I related heavily to it. The table was Nightmare Island, and its three chair were myself, Willow, and our unborn child. My father placed his hands on my shoulders and had me sit down, scooting me in before taking a seat himself.

They both were sad, yet smiles crept from the furthest corners of their mouths. I could see that they were happy. Why shouldn't they be? Their only child had died in their minds, yet there I was. Alive and in the flesh. I realized that I should try to put on a brave face, if only for them. It wasn't how I felt, but it was what they needed.

"How are you?" my mom said. Before I could answer, she said, "What am I saying? That's a stupid question. I'm sorry. This is just..." her voice cracked and trailed off and my father put his hand onto hers and gripped it lovingly.

"Damon, you have to understand," he said. "We thought...well...you know."

"Yeah, I know," I said somberly. "It's okay. I'm okay. I'm here."

"I wish we could've been there for you," my mom said through a burst of tears. I was silent, staring intently at the empty, frigidly of the steel grey table. The silence hung in the air like a thick fog. I knew they wanted to ask, but didn't know how. I understood that it couldn't be easy to ask the child you thought was dead about their mental breakdown. They probably thought I was crazy, running around the island like a feral pig with my imaginary friend.

"Can we just go home?" I asked. "I'm tired and really want to get some sleep."

"Of course, baby," my mom said placing her hands on the table, reaching out for me. I could tell she hoped that I would reach out for her, but I didn't. I just sat there, sulking in my misery. I loved my parents, but the love of my life was gone, forever. To me she was real, so because she was gone, it was almost like I mourned her, much like my parents mourned me.

I knew she wasn't real, but rather, was all in my mind. But, on Nightmare Island she was as real as the piercing sun rising in the east, full of color, promise, and warmth. With her gone, I was nothing. I was cold, pale, and empty. I was more alone than I had ever been.

DEREK E. KEELING

CHAPTER TWENTY TWO

"That's pretty much it," I said through a deep breath of air. "That was my time on Nightmare Island."

"Well, Damon, that certainly is an intense story," Dr. Eide said shuffling through her notepad. Over the course of a couple months Dr. Melanie Eide's notepad turned from a nice white legal pad to a mess of ink and scribbles. That single bundle of paper was the accumulation of everything on the island. More so, it was the only tangible piece of Willow that existed. Sure, she existed in my memories, but I felt that because she was in Dr. Eide's notepad, she was more real. It was as if the shear ink that made up the letters in her name brought her to life, no matter how minuscule. "Do you have any questions for me?" Dr. Eide asked.

"I just want to know," I said. "If Willow wasn't real the entire time, then how come I can remember her smell, her touch, her warmth?"

"The mind is a very powerful thing when it needs to be, Damon," she replied softly. "You talked in the beginning of our sessions about your feelings of committing suicide and how you even climbed up to the top of a cliff and were ready to do it. This, coupled with the trauma of a plane crash and possibly a traumatic brain injury forced your mind to protect itself. It created Willow so that you could survive. Self-preservation is a very strong force in your subconscious. Your brain created something to keep you alive, long before Willow. You talked about how something stalked you in the jungle. That was the beginning of your subconscious defending itself from your conscious mind's thoughts of death. It was trying to preserve itself by creating what you needed most, human contact."

"But, why would it just stalk me like that, instead of actually making a human present itself?" I asked, with a tinge of defensiveness.

"The mind is infinitely complicated," she said. "I would surmise that it was a sort of battle between the reality of your conscious mind and the self-preservation of your subconscious mind. It was only when your conscious mind gave up and gave into ending itself that your subconscious could take over and fully create what you needed to survive. In this case, it was Willow." Dr. Melanie Eide's office was adorned with numerous certificates that showed her knowledge of psychology. Even with all of that, it didn't make it any easier to believe what she said.

"I just can't believe that she never truly existed," I said. I felt a tear escape from my eye and roll down my cheek. I quickly wiped it with my shaking hand.

"She did exist, Damon," she said, putting her notepad down on the small table that separated us.

"What do you mean?" I said wiping away another runaway tear.

"On that island she was real," she said with a smile that revealed a perfect set of porcelain-white teeth. "Even though she didn't exist, like you or I, she was real to you. Like you said, you could smell her, feel her warmth, and together you both fell in love. For anyone, there's nothing more real than that. On that island, Damon, Willow was as real as you needed her to be."

"Is she still there?" I asked. "On Nightmare Island?"

"She will always be there, in spirit" she said. "But even more, she's in your heart, your memories, and she's changed who you are as a person. That's the single most important thing you need to remember. She will always be with you."

"But, I'll never get to see her again. Or hold her. Or hold our child," I said, each word forcing more tears from my eyes.

"I know," she said. "I'm sorry."

"Would she come back if I needed her again, like before?" I asked. I knew the question sounded crazy, but I had to know the answer.

"Unfortunately, it's not that easy," she said. "Even if you were under that much stress again you never know what your mind would create. It could create a completely different person. Or, it's possible that it could create Willow again, but it may not be her personality. There are so many variables I can't accurately answer that question. The key is to try and move on."

"I don't want to move on," I said through a shower of salty tears. "I want Willow."

"I understand," she said. "It's not going to be easy. I want to prescribe some medicine to help keep you calm. It'll relax you and can possibly help make things better now that you're back. It's not going to be easy, Damon. I won't sugarcoat it. It may take a long time to move away from these feelings, but you'll get there. Each day it will be easier and easier."

"What would happen if I just went back?" I said.

"Went back where?" she asked. "To the island?"

"Yeah," I answered. "What if I just went back to Nightmare Island?"

"I don't know, Damon," she said. "But I do know that it would not be a good idea. It wouldn't help you move forward. In fact, in would probably set you back quite a bit."

Her words were like ice, shattering all around me. I wanted her to just say that I could go back and Willow would be there, waiting for me. She would still be pregnant and everything would go back to the way it was. I didn't want medicine to dull me, I wanted to go home, to Willow.

My parents insisted that I stay at their house until I got back on my feet. Unfortunately, I had no one else to stay. They were really supportive, but I could tell that they thought I was broken. Their words were precise and aimed at not causing me any stress. I knew they had the best intention, but, for some reason, I hated it. I didn't blame them, but I felt like a ghost in the house. They had removed a shrine they created when they thought I was dead, but its spot was vacant.

"How was your visit with Melanie?" My mom asked.

"Who?" I said.

"Dr. Eide," she replied.

"Oh. It was okay," I said plainly.

"When do you see her next?" She asked.

"A week from today," I said. "She gave me this." I handed her the written prescription.

"Oh, okay," she said. "I can get this filled tomorrow for you."

"Okay, that sounds good," I replied. "I'm pretty tired. I think I'm just going to go to bed."

"Alright," she said, almost disappointed with my words. "You know that I love you, right, Damon?"

"Yes, I do," I said. "I love you, too."

As I laid in my bed I couldn't help but think of everything that happened. It rushed me with a fervent melancholy. Everything played over and over like a silent movie in my head. The plane, the baby getting sucked out of the cabin, Marvin, the unwedded woman, and, most of all, Willow and our unborn child. Nightmare Island still existed. It was a real place. My cabin was a real cabin. Maybe, I wondered, Willow is there, waiting for me. I knew what Dr. Eide said, but the idea that Willow could be there was so overwhelming I just couldn't shake it. I had to know. I had to return.

CHAPTER TWENTY THREE

I could see the island in the distance, jutting up like a mound of green velvet in the liquidness of the cerulean ocean. A gentle hum from the motor of the small fishing vessel permeated the humid tropical air.

I stood on the bow of the boat, staring wistfully at the island and its possibilities. I knew she had to be there, real or not. She was there. Waiting for me. Wondering where I've gone and if or when I would return.

"I'm coming, Willow," I whispered to myself. "I'm coming."

I told no one that I was leaving to return to the island. I planned for several weeks exactly how it would all work. I could never have asked my parents for money so that I could come back to the island, nor would they be likely to give it to me. I was surprised how quickly I was able to secure a personal cash loan to fund my journey. If they knew what I was planning on doing with the money, I imagine they never would've approved the loan. After all, I had no intentions of returning and paying it back.

I felt bad for sneaking away in the middle of the night, leaving my parents alone with their fears of dread, yet again. But, they would never understand. I assumed that they would figure it out once they realized that I was gone, but it was a chance I had to take. No one could possibly understand how much I love and care for Willow, and how much my soul yearned for her.

Almost as hard as leaving my mother and father was stepping back onto a plane for another flight. The fear of the plane crashing again and putting me somewhere else was frightening. Thankfully, the journey was met without issue. I found myself in Rarotonga, searching for a small boat to take me to Nightmare Island. It was strange. Before the plane crash, my plan was to solicit a boat for a journey to a deserted island for the length of one month, after which the boat would return and I would go home. While the situation was similar, it was all too different at the same time. Instead of one month, I was simply looking for a one-way trip to Nightmare Island.

I did plan a little better for my second and final trip, however. I brought with me a few items that would make survival relatively easier: a good quality machete, a couple small flint and steels, and a professional water filter.

"Sharks," the man piloting the boat said suddenly.

"What?" I said shaking my daze away.

"There are sharks right over there, see?" He said pointing to a grouping of shark fins protruding out from the water. I watched them swim in a menacing circle around our boat. I imagined they were the same sharks that feasted upon passengers of the plane crash.

The boat was rather small, but still needed to anchor away from the beach for fear of grounding itself. The captain lowered a small rubber dingy into the water and waved at me to get in. I grabbed my things, tossed them into the dingy, and made my way down the short ladder from the main boat into the rubber raft. I sat down and resumed my stare at the beach of Nightmare Island.

I gazed intently at every shape on the beach and on the jungle's edge, hoping for a glimpse of Willow. Unfortunately, I saw nothing. I hoped that maybe she was just in the cabin, or out foraging. Deep in my head, I knew she wasn't real in the literal sense, but that was irrelevant. If my mind could create her once, it could do it again. It had to do it again.

The captain climbed down into the dingy and started up the small trolling motor. The boat skirted along the calm flutter of waves leading up to the shore.

"So, you don't want me to return?" He asked in an awkward tone.

"No," I replied. "Someone else is coming to pick me up." I lied right to him. Truth was, I had no plans of anyone coming to get me, ever. But, for fear that he would return, lying seemed the best course of action. "Also, here, take this" I said handing him a few hundred dollar bills.

"What's this for?" He said surprisingly.

"If anyone asks about me, you never heard of me, saw me, or anything, okay?" I said with my eyes forward on the beach.

"You got it," he said. "I don't mean to pry, but are you sure you're going to be okay here? I mean, this place is pretty inhospitable."

"Trust me," I said confidently. "I'll be fine."

"Alright, then," he said slowing the boat down as we reached the shallow of the shore. "This is your stop then." I grabbed my stuff and hopped into the water, which soaked me up to my shins.

"Thank you," I said turning to the captain. "I appreciate it."

"No problem," he said. "You be safe here, okay?"

"You got it," I said. He gave me a quick salute and turned the dingy around and headed off towards his fishing boat.

I walked from the water, dropped my things off, and removed my soaked shoes. The sand felt like a blanket of cashmere beneath my feet. I had missed the silkiness of the sand between my toes and the gentle breeze of the saline ocean spray trickling its particles on my skin. I took in a single calming breath.

Scanning the shoreline and jungle's edge revealed nothing. No Willow. I began the trek toward our cabin, the home I had built for us. The jungle rung out with its normal perfume. It was almost overwhelming, but I relished its heady redolence. It brought back so many memories. The jungle seemed alive with birdsong. It created a symphony in the air that seemed to echo all around me. It was the jungle equivalent of Mozart, stunning, calming, and to be revered.

Through the jungle I could see the rough outline of our cabin. It stood tall and proud, like a beacon of hope. It did appear to have some jungle vines draping and clinging to its surface, but I thought that it seemed to give it a more natural character.

"Willow," I yelled at the cabin. I hoped and prayed that she would come out of the cabin and would run into my arms, asking where I was, and giving me guff for leaving her for so long. But, unfortunately, there was nothing. Just the sounds of birds, singing their day away.

I entered the cabin with haste, my heart beating with anticipation. It seemed that nothing had changed from the last time

I was there. Every single item was in the same spot, like nothing had been used.

"Willow," I yelled in the cabin. "It's me, Damon. Where are you?" No answer, except from the birds. It now seemed like they had gotten louder, as if they were purposely trying to drown out my calls. "Willow? Willow, I'm here. Are you there?" Again, nothing. Just the symphonic blast of feathered vermin. They conspired against me. I had no idea what to do. I wasn't sure why Willow wasn't showing herself. I thought of many horrible things. Maybe she would never come back. Maybe this was a horrible idea, just like Dr. Eide warned.

I stood and ran from the cabin and headed back through the jungle, hoping to run into to her as she was hunting. My heart pounded through my chest. My nerves were tied in knots.

"Willow!" I shrieked. "Where are you?" I ran through vines, bushes, and thorns, all the while shouting for her. I screamed her name more times than I can count and there wasn't a single replied.

I had to stop. I was running so hard that I needed to catch my breath. The jungle air went from lively and full of birdsong to bitter and betraying. My lungs burned, with either anger or lack of breath. At that point, I did not know. Sweat dripped profusely from my forehead.

"You have to be here, Willow," I said quietly to myself. "You just have to be. You have to." But then the thought of her not being here stung in my mind like a bee in the eye. It was bold, frightening, and stood my hair on end. If she wasn't here, and couldn't be here again, then I would truly be stuck here. This time I would certainly be alone.

"The boat," I said aloud. I sprang into action and ran as fast as I could for the beach. In no time I was standing again on the soft sands. In the far distance was the small shape of the fishing boat that brought me back to Nightmare Island.

"Hey," I screamed waving my hands. "Come back, please. Don't leave me here alone." I grabbed a fallen palm fronds and waved it as high as I could get it, but to no avail. The boat continued on into the distance until it completely disappeared. It was gone, probably forever, and I was then truly alone.

The skin on the back of my neck seemed to curl inwards and a foul feeling overtook my stomach. I told no one where I was. In fact, I had made every effort to ensure that no one knew for sure that this is where I came. I wanted to be left alone. Alone with Willow and our child. I hoped that we could've lived our lives together and be at peace, but instead I was all alone. Left to survive on Nightmare Island by myself.

I dropped to my knees, my hands gripping my face as tears poured from my eyes. I knew that it was only a matter of time before I found myself standing on the cliff again, looking down into my fate. Death. It was inevitable. Without Willow. Without anyone, I would die. I couldn't survive alone. Humans weren't meant to survive alone. We just weren't built to be by ourselves for too long. Without someone to be with, without Willow, I would die.

"Willow," I said quietly through a shower of tears. "I'm sorry. Why did I leave you? I'm so sorry."

Though the thick tangle of the jungle's mass of humid plants, the faint sound of a baby crying rang out through the air.

I was finally home.

ABOUT THE AUTHOR

Derek E. Keeling is an award winning journalist, author, content writer, and social media coordinator. He began his love of writing as a young teen and it has since flourished into a profound passion.

His work has been featured in numerous publications, including books, magazines, newspapers, blogs, websites, and more. He is the author of the noir mystery novel, The Umbras.

In his free time he enjoys spending time with his beautiful wife and daughter.

AMAZON: www.amazon.com/author/derekkeeling

FACEBOOK: www.facebook.com/keelingderek

INSTAGRAM: www.instagram.com/derekkeelingauthor

EMAIL: keelingderekauthor@gmail.com

PUBLISHED BY:

SALEM, OREGON

Made in the USA
Columbia, SC
11 February 2019